IT WAS MORE THAN A DESIRE—IT WAS AS IF SOME IRRESISTIBLE FORCE WAS DRAGGING THEM TOWARD THE WELL. . . .

Finally they reached the well and peered in.

The surface of the water was ripply, but below were clear lighted depths. At the bottom of the well they saw skeletons and drowned bodies, and among the pale corpses, they saw themselves, Anthony and Miss Eells, lying side by side in death.

Suddenly they felt themselves being grasped by powerful unseen hands. They tried to cry out, but they had no voices, and in spite of their frantic struggles they were dragged over the rough stone edge of the well curb and were thrust into the depths of the icy water. . . .

"Entertaining . . . Bellairs keeps the action moving."
—*Kirkus Reviews*

"Readers, particularly Bellairs's fans, should find [the book] engrossing." —*School Library Journal*

THE LAMP FROM
THE WARLOCK'S TOMB

JOHN BELLAIRS

Frontispiece
by Edward Gorey

A BANTAM SKYLARK BOOK®
NEW YORK · TORONTO · LONDON · SYDNEY · AUCKLAND

RL 6, 009–013

*This edition contains the complete text
of the original hardcover edition.*
NOT ONE WORD HAS BEEN OMITTED.

THE LAMP FROM THE WARLOCK'S TOMB

*A Bantam Skylark Book / published by arrangement with
Dial Books for Young Readers*

PRINTING HISTORY
Dial Books edition published December 1987

*Skylark Books is a registered trademark of Bantam Books,
a division of Bantam Doubleday Dell Publishing Group, Inc.
Registered in U.S. Patent and Trademark Office and elsewhere*

Bantam edition / May 1989

ISBN 0-553-15697-7

Published simultaneously in the United States and Canada

---

*Bantam Books are published by Bantam Books, a division of Bantam Doubleday Dell
Publishing Group, Inc. Its trademark, consisting of the words "Bantam Books" and the
portrayal of a rooster, is Registered in U.S. Patent and Trademark Office and in other
countries. Marca Registrada. Bantam Books, 666 Fifth Avenue, New York, New York 10103.*

PRINTED IN THE UNITED STATES OF AMERICA

S   0 9 8 7 6 5 4 3 2 1

The Lamp from
the Warlock's Tomb

CHAPTER ONE

"Hey, Miss Eells! Watch out!"

"Oh, calm down, Anthony. I may be clumsy, but I'm not all *that* clumsy! Why don't you go out to the car and read a road map till I'm through browsing in here? I hate to complain, but you are making me very nervous!"

On a sunny autumn day in the mid-1950's, Miss Myra Eells and her young friend, Anthony Monday, were poking around in an antique shop in the tiny Wisconsin town of Dresbach. Miss Eells was an odd, birdlike little woman with a messy nest of white hair and gold-rimmed spectacles. Anthony was tall and awkward-looking with a thin, pinched face and a long pointed nose. He wore a red leather cap with a scrunched peak all the time, indoors and out, in rainy weather and bright sunshine. Right now Anthony was looking worried, as he always did when he and Miss Eells were in antique shops. Miss Eells was the sort of person who could knock valuable china dishes off a table with a sweep of her arm, or shatter Chinese urns by stumbling up against them. Anthony was always afraid that she would break something that was fantastically expensive and then have to spend the rest of her life paying for it. At present Miss Eells was standing in a narrow space between two big old dining room tables that were loaded with fragile-looking things: china cups and saucers, glass vases, medicine bottles, and oil lamps. She was moving her hands over the objects on the table as if she were a magician getting ready to do some enchantment. Suddenly she swooped down and grabbed an oil lamp. It was really quite beautiful: The base was made of beaded ruby-red glass, and the slender curved chimney was fitted with a pink outer globe that had cabbage roses painted on it. Miss Eells was crazy about oil lamps—she had several in her home, and she was always saying that some year she would turn off the electricity and live the way they did in the horse-and-buggy days, just for fun.

Anthony was getting more nervous by the minute. He watched as Miss Eells swung the fragile-looking lamp, making the outer globe rattle and squeak.

"For gosh sakes, Miss Eells!" he burst out. "Be careful! You might—"

But Miss Eells had had enough of Anthony's *nittiness*. "Anthony Monday, you stop all this right now!" she exclaimed indignantly. "Good Lord, you'd think I was ten years old and you were my mother! It's true that I stick my foot into wastebaskets now and then, but I have some really valuable and fragile objects in my home, and somehow I have managed to—"

At this point Miss Eells took a step backward, and as she did this, she jammed her right elbow against a tall bureau that was standing nearby. Her arm went numb and the fingers of her right hand flew apart. For an agonizing second she juggled the lamp, but then it fell to the floor with a loud crash.

Horrified, Miss Eells and Anthony stared down at the wreckage. The owner had been up on the second floor, but now the sound of her footsteps echoed on the hall stairs as she returned. Anthony and Miss Eells braced themselves for a scene—what on earth would Adele Grimshaw say? Would she yell at them and demand payment? Miss Eells reached down with her right hand and felt for the checkbook in her purse, which lay on the table. She had a feeling that she would need it.

The hall door opened, and the owner, a frowning, middle-aged woman with dyed brown stringy hair, stepped in. Mrs. Grimshaw always talked in a flat, monotonous voice, and she acted as if she had never gotten any fun out of life. Now, as Mrs. Grimshaw stood staring down at the shattered oil lamp, Anthony braced himself for an explosion. But none came. Amazingly, Mrs. Grimshaw was quite calm, and once or twice Anthony thought that she was actually going to smile. But each time the smile started, she coughed and wiped her hand across her mouth.

"I'm really *awfully* sorry," said Miss Eells in a distressed voice. "I was just bragging to my friend here about how careful I was being, but I guess the gods of clumsiness were listening and decided to punish me. I can pay for—"

"Oh, that won't be necessary," said Mrs. Grimshaw with a careless wave of her hand. "To tell the truth, I have never liked that lamp. Myra, why don't I get a broom and a dustpan, and then you and I can go upstairs and find a lamp that you might want to buy. How does that sound?"

Miss Eells was astounded. She knew Mrs. Grimshaw pretty well, and she had always thought that the woman was an incredible fussbudget. But here she was, shrugging her shoulders when a valuable oil lamp got smashed to smithereens. It was all pretty strange, and alarm bells began to ring in Miss Eells's mind. There's something wrong here, she said to herself, but she managed to smile politely and thank the woman for being so understanding. Anthony heaved a deep sigh of relief.

A few minutes later, Miss Eells, Mrs. Grimshaw, and Anthony were up in one of the rooms on the second floor. Chattering nervously, the owner led her two customers past some stacked boxes to an old marble-topped bureau. A carved wooden screen rose from the top of the bureau, and it held a wooden box that looked like a medicine chest. As Miss Eells and Anthony watched, Mrs. Grimshaw opened the door to the front of the chest and took out a small oil lamp. As soon as Miss Eells saw the lamp, she fell in love with it. The chimney was a slender curved vase of blown glass, and on the base were little Dutch scenes painted in blue on milky-white china. Windmills, a low fence near a grassy dune, a canal boat with a fisherman sitting on the bow—Anthony and Miss Eells saw all these as Mrs. Grimshaw slowly turned the lamp around. It's wonderful! thought Miss Eells, but then another thought occurred to her: Why had the owner of the antique shop kept this beautiful lamp up here, shut inside a dark cabinet?

"Do you like it?" asked Mrs. Grimshaw as she turned the lamp back and forth in her hands.

In spite of the doubts and fears that kept flitting through her mind, Miss Eells had to admit that she was fascinated by the lamp. She imagined it sitting on the oval antique table next to her living room sofa. But Miss Eells knew that Mrs. Grimshaw would jack the price up if she acted too enthusiastic.

"Why . . . why, yes, it's quite nice," murmured Miss

Eells as calmly as she could. "How much do you want for it?"

When the owner told her the price, Miss Eells's mouth dropped open. It was unbelievably cheap! *Why?* Why was the woman selling this lovely antique lamp for such a low price?

Miss Eells turned to Anthony. "What do you think, Tony?"

Anthony frowned and shrugged. "It's okay, I guess. I don't know anything about antiques, so I guess I'm a bad person to ask."

Miss Eells hesitated. She really loved the lamp, but something inside was telling her to watch out. Finally she heaved a deep sigh, grinned, and unsnapped the top of her purse. "I'll take it," she said excitedly. "I shouldn't spend the money, but I really can't resist. It's one of the prettiest antique oil lamps I've ever seen."

"Yes, isn't it?" said Mrs. Grimshaw in an odd voice. "Come downstairs and I'll wrap it up for you."

So Anthony and Miss Eells followed Mrs. Grimshaw downstairs to the counter at the front of the shop. Miss Eells wrote out a check, and the owner packed the lamp into a cardboard box and stuffed in wads of newspaper to keep the lamp from rattling around on the trip home. Then Miss Eells said good-bye, and she and Anthony went out to her car and drove off.

The road back to Hoosac ran along the eastern bank

of the Mississippi River, and on the left tall limestone bluffs loomed. As they drove along, Miss Eells and Anthony were strangely silent. The box with the lamp in it lay on the seat between them, and every now and then Miss Eells glanced nervously at it. Then she would force herself to forget about the box and go back to staring at the road.

The sun went down, and the twilight deepened into night. Headlights came on, and still they drove. Neither of them said a word.

"What are you thinking about, Anthony?" asked Miss Eells suddenly. The sound of her own voice startled her—it seemed high-pitched and squeaky.

"I'm thinking about the dumb lamp you bought," said Anthony sullenly. "How come Mrs. Whosis hid it away inside a chest? If she liked it, wouldn't she want to show it off?"

"You would think so," said Miss Eells thoughtfully. "On the other hand, maybe she liked the lamp so much that she hid it and hoped that no one would buy it. But then why did she rush up and dig it out for us when I broke that other lamp? The whole incident is really weird when you come to think of it."

"Yeah," muttered Anthony as he scratched his ear. "Maybe Mrs. Whosis is—oh my gosh! Look out!"

Straight ahead a man was standing in the middle of the road. With a yell Miss Eells swerved the car sharply to the right. When she jammed on the brakes, the car skidded sideways over crackling gravel and came to a stop near a row of wooden posts.

"Heavenly days!" gasped Miss Eells. "What on *earth* do you suppose that fool was doing out there in the middle of the road?"

Anthony scowled. "I dunno," he said, "but I'm gonna go out and give him a piece of my mind."

Before Miss Eells could do anything to stop him, Anthony was out of the car and walking boldly along the gravelly shoulder of the road. He stopped just beyond the glare of the headlights and cupped his hands to his mouth.

"Hey you!" he yelled. "What the heck're you doin'? You might've got us all killed!"

Silence. Anthony peered into the darkness, and he found that he could just barely make out a short man, who seemed to be wearing a long black overcoat. The man started walking toward the side of the road, and Anthony followed him. A full moon had just risen over the tall shadowy bluffs, and by its light Anthony saw the man disappear into a little clump of trees. Anthony hesitated. He knew it was dangerous to follow the man, but he was angry. With long strides Anthony moved toward the trees, but then suddenly he stopped. A chill seized his body, and he trembled violently. He felt a sickening, numbing fear. For about a minute Anthony just stood there shaking with his eyes closed. Then the chill passed and he forced his eyes to open. After a quick fearful glance at the dark mass of boughs, Anthony turned and ran back to the car.

"Good Lord!" exclaimed Miss Eells as he jerked the car door open. "Anthony, that was an *unbelievably* foolish thing to do! That man might have had a knife or a gun, and you could have gotten yourself killed!"

Anthony slumped into his seat and folded his arms. He was struggling hard to hide his fear. "Aw, he was just a creepy little guy in an overcoat," he muttered disdainfully.

Miss Eells gave Anthony an exasperated glance and, with an anxious sigh, she turned the ignition key and revved up the engine. "Maybe you could have handled that man," she said quietly. "But on the other hand, maybe you couldn't have. Is your door locked? Good! Hang on, because we are going to burn some rubber!"

And with that, Miss Eells threw the car into gear and roared off in a cloud of smoke. As they drove back to Hoosac, Miss Eells and Anthony did not say much. When Anthony finally got out of the car in front of his house, he felt depressed and fearful. He was worried about Miss Eells. This made no sense, because he was the one who had been in danger a few minutes ago, not her. Nevertheless, he was afraid that something would happen to her. Silently Anthony told himself that he was being silly. Miss Eells was always in danger because she was a clumsy person, yet somehow she had made it almost to the age of seventy. Probably she would survive for another day or two, at least. Anthony forced himself to smile and wave good-bye cheerfully, but as Miss Eells drove off he felt a stab of fear again. Why was he worried?

Weeks passed, and life went on as usual for Anthony. During the day he went to classes at Hoosac High School, and in the evenings he worked at the public library. Miss Eells was the head librarian there, and she had hired Anthony a few years ago because she liked him and wanted to do something that would make Anthony feel better about himself. Since then, Anthony and Miss Eells had gotten to be close friends. They played chess, and Anthony told her things he would never have told his mother. And when things were slow at the library, the two of them would just sit around and gossip and enjoy each other's company. It was an odd friendship, but it worked.

One gray November afternoon, Anthony walked into the Hoosac Public Library and immediately started looking for Miss Eells. She wasn't hard to find: She was on her knees in front of the fireplace in the East Reading Room, trying unsuccessfully to build a fire. Heaps of burnt matches littered the hearthstone, and the mouth of the fireplace was stuffed with wads of scorched newspaper. As Anthony watched, Miss Eells tried to strike a match on the sandpapered side of the box she held in her hands. But the match broke in two, and the flaring tip landed on the hem of her dress. Swearing angrily, she beat the flame out with her hands and then turned to glare up at Anthony. Her face was red and she was breathing heavily.

"*Well?*" she said.

Anthony didn't know what to say. Usually Miss Eells was pretty easygoing, and he enjoyed talking to her. But today he had a favor to ask of her, and he began to think that maybe this was not the time to ask for favors.

Suddenly Miss Eells laughed. The hard lines of her face relaxed, and she shook her head slowly. "I'm sorry I snapped at you, Tony," she said, still chuckling. "But I'm in one of my firebug moods. Maybe someday I will chop the library furniture into kindling wood and burn the place down, and that will convince people that I'm not to be trusted with matches." She sighed. "I think you look like someone who wants to ask a favor. Am I right?"

Anthony was amazed. Miss Eells was the sort of person who couldn't open a can of beans without cutting her hand to ribbons, but she always knew what was on his mind.

Slowly, with lots of hemming and hawing, Anthony explained. His physics class was doing a project for the science fair that was going to be held in a week. He and some friends were planning an exhibit that demonstrated old-fashioned methods of lighting. One boy was making a replica of a Roman clay lamp, and a girl was making a Colonial rush lamp. Anthony had said that he would get hold of a kerosene lamp for the project. At first he had planned to bring one from his own home, but his mother was worried that the lamp would get broken, so she had refused to let him have it. Now he was turning to Miss Eells for help.

". . . and we won't hurt it, I promise," said Anthony. "We'll only need it for a little while and I'll be the only one who's allowed to—"

"Oh for heaven's sake, Anthony, stop begging!" said Miss Eells in an exasperated voice. "You can have the lamp! I'll be *delighted* to let you take it!" Then she smiled strangely and added, in an odd voice, "To tell you the truth, I've never taken it out of its box. When was it that I bought the lamp? A month ago, I think. Well, ever since then it's been lying in a corner of my living room like a mummy in a coffin. I guess that I didn't like it as much as I thought I did. In any case, it's yours to use. And if you should accidentally drop it out a third-story window . . . well, I think I'd probably forgive you."

Anthony stared blankly at Miss Eells. Something very odd was going on, that was for certain. He remembered how Miss Eells had oohed and aahed over the lamp in Mrs. Grimshaw's antique shop. What had made her change her mind?

Anthony worked at the library till closing time, as

usual, and Miss Eells offered to give him a ride home. On the way, they were going to stop by her house so that he could pick up the lamp. As they rode along, Anthony told Miss Eells that he thought she looked tired.

"Funny you should mention it," said Miss Eells, smiling wryly. "Tony, I haven't been getting a lot of sleep lately. I keep waking up and imagining that I hear things. Once I thought I had left a radio on downstairs, but when I went down to check, they were all turned off. And another time I thought someone was rattling the front door—but I guess it was just the wind."

"It might've been burglars," said Anthony nervously. "My mom says that break-ins are on the increase everywhere, and—"

"Oh, your *mother*!" said Miss Eells, laughing. "She must sit up nights worrying about all the ghastly things that could happen to the people she knows. No, my friend. It's not burglars, it's too many cups of coffee late at night. I'm having Sanka this evening, and then I'm going to hit the sack with a loud thud and sleep till my alarm goes off at eight o'clock."

When they got to Miss Eells's house, she went inside and brought out the white china lamp. It was still neatly packed in its box, and the top of the box was sealed with masking tape. With the box on his lap, Anthony rode back to his house with Miss Eells.

"Keep it as long as you like," said Miss Eells with a

careless shrug. "I suspect that I spent all that money for nothing. I mean, it's really a rather ugly lamp, isn't it? Well, see you tomorrow."

And with that she rolled up the car window and drove off. Once again a dark, shapeless worry began to form in Anthony's mind. He looked down at the box in his hands and frowned. Then he sighed and told himself that there was nothing to worry about, nothing in all the world.

CHAPTER TWO

A week later, around eight o'clock on a Tuesday night, Anthony was in the chemistry lab of the high school. All around him students were setting up their own exhibits. One group was working on a display of glass tubes filled with gases that glowed different colors when an electrical current was passed through them; another bunch of kids was making a dust explosion inside a potato chip can; and still another was setting up an induction coil. Anthony was all by himself at a long marble-topped table—the other boy, who was supposed to help him make signs for the exhibit, had not shown up. All the pieces of the exhibit were there: the red clay lamp that burned vegetable oil, the rush light with its long, thin taper, a candle that was banded to show different times of the day as it burned, and the oil lamp that Anthony had borrowed from Miss Eells. With an art pen in his hand and a bottle of black India ink nearby, Anthony carefully lettered the signs that were going to be used for the exhibit. Every now and then he would glance up at the Dutch china lamp that burned quietly nearby. The slender chimney was filled with a yellow-ish glow, and little wisps of black smoke coiled up steadily. Anthony had fussed with the little wheel that adjusted the wick until he had the lamp burning just the way he wanted it. But he did not plan to keep it going very long—he didn't have an extra supply of wicks, and he wanted the lamp to burn for at least an hour on the day of the exhibit, which was tomorrow. He was proud of the lamp—at least he tried to be. But he had begun to understand the way Miss Eells felt: There really was something unpleasant about this odd little antique object. Anthony couldn't have said why he disliked the lamp, but he would be glad when the exhibit was over with and he could take it back to his friend.

The door at the far end of the lab slammed three or four times—the other students were starting to leave. Anthony labored on, moving his pen slowly over the white cardboard.

"Hey, Tony! Come on! Let's knock off and go down to Swenson's for an ice cream," said Ted Hoopenbecker, a big, red-haired kid who was sort of a friend of Anthony's.

Anthony looked up and sighed. "You go ahead, Ted," he muttered sadly. "I've still got two more of these signs to do. I'll be down there a little later."

"Right, kid! Don't work too hard!" And with that Ted was gone, closing the door behind him. Anthony looked around: He was alone in the lab now. He shrugged and went back to work, dipping his pen in the black ink. Anthony was a loner—he didn't mind doing things by himself. But as he worked, the silence of the dark, closed-up high school building grew on him. He imagined that he heard doors opening and shutting in the distance. In his mind's eye he saw shadowy figures walking up and down the long moonlit corridors that lay beyond the lighted room he was in. The flame of the oil lamp began to flicker, which was odd, because there wasn't any draft, and the glass chimney was there to protect the flame. Anthony reached out to twiddle the adjusting wheel, but as he did, somebody knocked on the door.

Anthony jumped. He lurched forward and nearly knocked over the lamp, but luckily he grabbed it in time and set it back on its base. Then he turned and went to answer the door. When he opened it, he heaved a sigh of relief—it was Mr. Yurchak, the night watchman. He was a short, fat, elderly man in a rumply blue uniform, and he smoked the worst-smelling cigars in the world. Anthony liked Mr. Yurchak because he was pretty easy-going.

"Hi, Tony!" wheezed Mr. Yurchak cheerfully. "Burnin' the midnight oil, eh?"

Anthony glanced back over his shoulder at the lamp. He didn't know whether Mr. Yurchak was trying to be funny or not. "Yeah, I guess you could say that," he muttered, smiling wryly. "I have to make all these signs, and it's takin' a pretty long time. But I'll be outta here in another five minutes."

"I'll time ya," chuckled Mr. Yurchak, and he winked. With a cheerful wave, he turned away. Then he stopped—he had remembered something. "Oh, by the way, Tony," he added, pointing down the dark corridor, "when ya come out, use the main door. All o' the other ones're locked up tight. I'll be out in front o' the buildin', havin' a smoke."

"Okay, Mr. Yurchak," said Anthony, and he closed the door softly. His shoes squeaked as he walked back to the lab table. Why did he feel so depressed? An awful heaviness lay upon him, like the feeling you have when someone close to you has died. Grimly Anthony picked up the pen and started making letters again. Five mintues passed—it seemed like hours—but finally he was done. Heaving a deep sigh, Anthony corked the ink bottle and wiped the pen dry. As he put out the lamp, his hand happened to brush the white china base, and he was startled by the chill he felt from it. This was very odd—the lamp had been burning for some time, and the base ought to have been warm. But Anthony wasn't going to hang around and brood about the lamp—his job was done and he was going home. Whistling softly, he picked up the flashlight he had brought with him and strode to the door. He turned off the room lights and stepped out into the hall.

Down the long corridor he walked, playing the beam of his flashlight all around. Anthony had been in the high school at night before, when he tried out for the school basketball team, but he had never been this nervous. The classroom doors were locked tight, but he kept expecting them to fly open as he passed. This is ridiculous, he told himself, but ridiculous or not, he felt scared. He went down the wide, slippery staircase and along the shadowy main corridor toward the entrance. Squeak, squeak went his sneakers on the waxed tile floor. He passed the glimmering windows of the school office, pushed open the heavy door, and stepped out into the high columned porch. Where was Mr. Yurchak? Anthony flashed the pale ray of his light off to the right, and suddenly his blood froze.

He was staring at a man, a short man in a long black overcoat with tattered edges. The man's pale, freckled head was bald, and his eyes were small, cruel, and beady. Across the man's face stretched a crisscrossing mass of black strands—they looked like spider webs.

Anthony screamed. He dropped his flashlight and rushed blindly out between two columns. Something large lay in his path, and he tripped over it and went sprawling. As he scrambled to his feet he glanced back and saw what he had fallen over—it was the body of Mr. Yurchak, who was lying on his face. Blind panic gripped Anthony, and he ran. He dashed two blocks over to Main Street and kept on running till he saw the blue light outside the door of the police station, which was on the ground floor of the City Hall. The sergeant at the desk looked up and gaped in astonishment as he saw Anthony reel in through the door: He was wild-eyed, red-faced, and panting.

"Police! Help! He's *dead*!" gasped Anthony as he staggered forward and grabbed the top of the high desk. His legs felt weak, and he had a pounding headache. "It's true! Please *believe me*!" he yelled.

But for the time being, the policeman just stared.

CHAPTER THREE

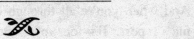

It took some time for Anthony to calm down. The desk sergeant led him to a chair and gave him a glass of water. Haltingly, between sips, Anthony explained what had happened. At first the sergeant was puzzled and a bit suspicious. Was this a high school prank of some sort? Well (he told himself) if it was, Anthony was a pretty darned good actor. So the sergeant went to a desk with a microphone on it and contacted one of the patrol cars. He asked them to go to the high school and see if there was a dead body on the front steps. A few minutes later the report from the patrol car came back, and as the sergeant listened over the headphones, his eyes grew wide and his mouth dropped open.

"*Huh?*" he exclaimed. "Are you *sure?* Hey, you guys aren't tryin' to put one over on me, are you? All right, all right . . . don't get mad. Look, maybe you better call the coroner's office. Then get some detectives down to the high school to look for clues, and have the body sent to the county morgue so they can do an autopsy. And when you're all through over there, come in and file a report. Ten-four, over and out."

The sergeant switched off the mike and got up slowly. He turned to Anthony, who wanted to cry, though he tried hard to fight back the tears. "Well, kid," the sergeant muttered, "you were right. I'll tell you one thing: There's gonna be one heck of a story in the newspaper tomorra."

And quite a story it was. The next morning the Hoosac *Daily Sentinel* ran it on the front page under the heading GHOULISH DEATH AT HIGH SCHOOL. The article told how two patrolmen had found the body of Mr. Stanislas Yurchak lying facedown on the steps outside the Hoosac High School building. Mr. Yurchak's body was in pretty horrible shape: The skin was white and papery and shrunken on the bones, and over Mr. Yurchak's face a crisscrossing net of thick black cobwebs was spread. No one could explain how Mr. Yurchak's body had gotten in such a shocking condition, but an autopsy would be held, and that might provide some answers. The article also mentioned that Anthony Monday, a student at the high school, had found the body. He had been questioned, but no one felt that he had had anything to do with the murder.

"Well, it's so nice of them to say that!" said Mrs. Monday sarcastically. She laid the paper down on the kitchen table and shook her head sadly. Anthony's mother was very crabby, and she was always worrying about what the neighbors thought of her. "You don't think they'll connect Anthony with this horrible murder, do you, Howard?" she asked plaintively. "I mean, he just found the poor man. He couldn't possibly have done all those awful things to him!"

Mr. Monday put his coffee cup down. "Look," he said wearily, "nobody is gonna charge Anthony with *anything*. They've got enough on their hands tryin' to figure out what happened to old Yurchak. Maybe it's some kinda disease that nobody knows about. Maybe that's what happened to him."

"I hope Anthony doesn't catch it," muttered Mrs. Monday, glancing nervously at her son. "Do you feel all right, Tony?"

Anthony stuffed a forkful of scrambled eggs into his mouth and chewed them slowly. "I'm okay, Mom," he said between chews. "Only I don't think Mr. Yurchak had any kind of a disease. Something awful happened to him."

"Did you see anybody hangin' around the high school last night?" asked Mr. Monday.

Anthony stared grimly at his plate. "No," he said. "I

didn't see anybody but the kids who were workin' in the chemistry lab with me."

Mr. and Mrs. Monday went on talking about the death of Mr. Yurchak, but Anthony clammed up. He had not told his parents, or the police, or anyone, about the strange man who had been standing inside the porch of the high school. He hated to lie, but he was convinced that he had seen a ghost, and people thought you were nutty if you talked to them about ghosts. Unfortunately, the lie he had told was burning a hole in his brain—he had to tell someone the truth, and of course that someone was Miss Eells. She had always listened to him, and he was sure she would listen to him now.

The science exhibit at the high school was postponed because of Mr. Yurchak's death, and a large number of students turned up at his funeral. Anthony rode out to the cemetery with Miss Eells, and after the graveside ceremony, the two of them ambled down one of the gravel paths that wound among the fields of headstones. As they walked, Anthony told Miss Eells the true story of the things he had seen on the night of Mr. Yurchak's death. He threw in a lot of odd details that didn't seem to matter: the nervous feeling he had had when he was alone in the chemistry lab, and the peculiar way the oil lamp had flickered. Miss Eells listened intently as Anthony talked, and now and then she threw a sharp sidelong glance at him. When he began talking about the oil lamp she stopped on the path and picked up a handful of dry leaves. Crumbling them, she let the brown dust sift through her fingers. Finally she spoke.

"Anthony, what are you saying? Are you trying to tell me that you think there's some connection between the lamp and that weird man you saw?"

Anthony nodded. "That's right, Miss Eells. I know it sounds crazy, but . . . well, do you remember the man that was standin' in the road when we were comin' back from the antique shop? We saw him right after you bought the lamp, and he looked just like the guy that was hidin' in the high school porch. And the lamp was at the high school too."

Miss Eells made a sour face. "Anthony, my dear friend," she said, "you're a great boy and you have many fine qualities, but you get Z minus in logic. If it rains after I have flapped my nylons out the bedroom window, that doesn't mean that it has rained *because* of what I did. There doesn't have to be any connection between the web-faced man and the oil lamp. Besides, you didn't get a good look at the man in the road. How can you be so sure that he's the man you saw at the high school?"

"I'm not sure," said Anthony sullenly, and he kicked at a pile of leaves. "But I'll tell you one thing. That guy at the high school wasn't alive. He was a ghost or something like that. Real live people don't have cobwebs all over their faces."

Miss Eells smiled. "No, they don't," she said thoughtfully. "Unless, of course, they live in attics that are infested with spiders. I'm not trying to make fun of you, Anthony. But the man who murdered Mr. Yurchak might have been wearing some sort of hideous Halloween makeup so that people wouldn't recognize him. And, of course, if people want to think that he's a ghost and not alive, so much the better for him. Do you see what I mean?"

Anthony bit his lip. "Yeah, I do," he muttered, "but I still think you're wrong. What about the shape that Mr. Yurchak's body was in? Doesn't that prove that a ghost killed him?"

Miss Eells pursed her lips and shook her head. "Not necessarily. There are lots of weird poisons in the world, and the Hoosac County Coroner's Office probably hasn't heard of them all. What did the newspaper say? Death due to unknown causes, I think. You don't have to drag in a supernatural explanation—though I will admit one thing: Mr. Yurchak's body was in pretty horrible shape."

They walked on in silence for a while, and then Anthony spoke again. "What I can't figure out," he said, "is why anybody would want to kill Mr. Yurchak. He was a really nice old guy. Of course if it was a ghost—which is what I still think—he wouldn't need a reason, would he? I mean, in the old stories that you read . . ."

Anthony's voice trailed away. In the distance, beyond the iron fence that bordered the cemetery, someone was pacing back and forth. It was Mrs. Grimshaw, the woman from the antique shop.

When Miss Eells saw what Anthony was looking at, she gasped in astonishment. "Good night!" she exclaimed. "What on *earth* is she doing here?"

Anthony was silent. Some wild ideas were running through his head, but he didn't want to talk about them. "Maybe she's a friend of Mr. Yurchak's," he said at last. "I mean, maybe she came here to pay her last respects."

Miss Eells shook her head. "No," she said firmly. "Adele doesn't have many friends, and I really doubt that old Stan was the kind of person she would sit around playing gin rummy with. No, Anthony, but it is strange that she's here. However, I'd rather not talk to her now. There's a side gate to this cemetery, and I think we ought to use it. Come on!"

Miss Eells led Anthony to a fancy iron archway where they ran quickly across the street and plunged in behind a row of cypress trees. From there it was only three blocks to Miss Eells's car, which was parked next to a fire hydrant. A ticket had been tucked neatly under one of the car's windshield wipers.

With a disdainful snort, Miss Eells folded the ticket in two and tucked it into her purse. "Humph!" she said sourly. "You would think the police would have better things to do with their time than to hand out tickets to people who are attending funerals. Oh, well. At least we managed to avoid the Dragon Lady. Let's head back to the library and see what damage we can do there!"

As they drove off, Miss Eells noticed that Anthony

was in a very bad mood. He kept biting his lip, and he stared moodily out the side window of the car. They drove for several blocks, but still he said nothing. Finally Miss Eells could stand it no longer.

"Anthony Monday!" she exclaimed in exasperation. "Are you still thinking about that dratted lamp?"

Anthony nodded grimly.

Miss Eells swerved quickly into the parking lot of a restaurant and stopped. She turned off the motor and sat back with her arms folded. "Look, my friend," she said slowly, "there is only one way to handle this problem. Where is that stupid oil lamp?"

Anthony looked startled. "It . . . it's up in the chemistry lab," he said hesitantly. "That's where I left it so we could use it for the exhibit."

Miss Eells grinned and she laid her hand on Anthony's arm. "Fine!" she said triumphantly. "Excellent! Now, when school opens tomorrow, why don't you put it in your locker, and then after school you can bring it to the library. I'll put it on top of the fireplace in the East Reading Room, and light it every evening for a week. You'll see that there's absolutely nothing to be afraid of. That lamp is about as magical as my grandmother's toothbrush. Soon you'll be laughing at all your fears, and you'll be able to get a good night's sleep. I mean, really! Haunted oil lamps, my foot!"

CHAPTER FOUR

Anthony still had some deep fears and suspicions about the oil lamp, but Miss Eells kept telling him he was being silly, and finally he began to think that maybe she was right. The day after Mr. Yurchak's funeral, Anthony went to the chemistry lab of the high school, packed the lamp in its cardboard box, and took it over to the library. The East Reading Room had a very fancy fireplace with a hand-carved screen over the broad marble mantel, and it was on the mantel that Miss Eells placed the lamp. Then she got a long white wax taper, lit it, and thrust it down the chimney to light the wick. The lamp glowed, and Miss Eells beamed with satisfaction.

"You see, Anthony?" she said as she climbed down

from the stool she had been standing on. "It's just a lovely old lamp and nothing more. Now you start shelving books, and I'll go back to work on that stupid card catalog. After a week has passed, you will think that all your fears were totally silly!"

Days passed. Every evening, after school, Anthony would walk in through the front door of the library and glance past the large carved archway to see if the lamp was still there. It always was, and it was always burning brightly. So far nothing odd had happened. However, on the last few evenings, when he and Miss Eells were closing up the library, Anthony had heard some unexplained noises. The library building was large and cavernous, with smoking rooms and lounges on the second and third floors. There was also one long parlor that held the private collection of Alpheus T. Winterborn, the man who had donated the money used to build the library. As part of his routine, Anthony had to take his master key and go make sure the doors of all these rooms were locked. Once or twice, when he was doing this, he had heard scuffling sounds inside the rooms, and he even thought that he heard someone laugh. But each time, when he opened the door, there was no one there.

On a rainy Thursday night Anthony walked into the library and saw—to his great relief—that the lamp was gone. Miss Eells was sitting at the main desk, and when she saw him she grinned.

"I'll bet you think I smashed it, don't you?" she said, staring hard at him and grinning even more widely.

Anthony blushed. "Nope," he said, shaking his head vigorously. "I just . . . well, I kind of wondered what happened to it."

Miss Eells sighed. "Well, it seems that Mrs. Oxenstern was in the other day, and she claimed that the fumes of the lamp were making her ill. I decided that I would humor her just this once, so I took the lamp to my office, and it's there, burning away merrily. Don't worry—I've got the window open, so I won't die of carbon monoxide poisoning. Now I wonder if—"

"Miss Eells, put the lamp out. *Please!*" said Anthony suddenly. He had turned pale, and he was glancing around nervously, as if he expected dark things to come rushing at him out of the shadowy corners of the library.

Miss Eells was startled, but then she set her mouth in a stubborn frown and folded her arms. "No, Anthony," she said slowly, "I'm not going to do that. I refuse to allow you to turn us both into nervous wrecks just because of that silly lamp. I said I'd keep the lamp burning every night for one week, and one week it's going to be. After that I'll take the thing home with me and we'll both be cured of this idiotic phobia. And while I remember—I'd better go back to my office and give the lamp some more oil." And with that she slid off her seat and hurried down the corridor.

It seemed like a long evening of work for Anthony. The hours dragged past, and he found that he kept glancing up at the clock over the main entrance. Usually he enjoyed his job at the library, but tonight, for some reason, he couldn't wait to get back to his house and shut the front door behind him. Twice he had been startled to see an old man in a long overcoat walking around on the upper level of the stacks. But it had only been Mr. Beemis, a secretive little character who spent about six nights a week in the library, aimlessly leafing through books and magazines. Anthony was a pretty courageous kid, and he was ashamed of being so jittery. He kept telling himself that Miss Eells was right about the lamp. Finally, as nine o'clock approached, he found that he was beginning to calm down. The evening was nearly over, and nothing bad had happened. Soon he would be sitting in front of the television set with a baloney sandwich and a Coke, and everything would be fine.

On the front steps of the library, Anthony said good night to Miss Eells. The rain had stopped, but a clammy, clinging chill hung in the air, and Anthony shivered a bit as he handed the library keys to his friend.

"So much for fearsome spectres," said Miss Eells cheerfully as she dumped the keys into her purse. "We've burned the evil lamp for six whole days, and so far no ghouls or goblins have materialized. I'm sorry that you didn't want to tell the police about the man you saw hiding on the night Mr. Yurchak was murdered. He might just have been a weird old bum, but then again, he might have been the one who—"

"He's the one who killed Mr. Yurchak," said Anthony, cutting her off. "But he's not alive, and you can't throw ghosts in jail. Someday you'll realize that I'm right, Miss Eells—you really will."

Miss Eells shrugged helplessly. She liked Anthony a lot, and she didn't want to get into an argument with him. "All right, all right, maybe it *was* a ghost," she said softly. "But I don't think there's any reason why we should stand here arguing on this nasty cold evening. Go home and sleep, and I'll see you tomorrow."

"G'night, Miss Eells," muttered Anthony, and he forced himself to smile. Then he shoved his hands into the pockets of his leather jacket and trotted on down the stone steps.

With his mind full of tangled and bizarre thoughts, Anthony plodded home. The Monday house was ten blocks away, but Anthony was a good walker, and he didn't mind the long hike. As he crossed Exchange Street, Anthony peered down a dark alley toward a little antique shop that he had always liked. It was run by a big hulking gray-haired man named Sven Magnusson, and the wide display window was always full of fascinating old-fashioned things that Anthony liked to look at. Today as he passed the entrance of the alley, Anthony was surprised to see that a light was on inside. Not a night-light, but a strong, bright open-for-business light that threw a pale yellow slash across the muddy little street. Anthony wondered what was going on, because he knew Mr. Magnusson was a person who kept regular nine-to-five hours. Oh well, he thought, maybe he's taking an inventory or something. With a shrug Anthony started to walk on, but then he stopped. For some reason he wanted to take a peek at the shop, so he turned on his heel and marched on down the alley to the far end.

As he stumbled along among the ruts and puddles, Anthony wondered why it was so important for him to go down and investigate the lighted window. To tell the truth, he felt *compelled*, as if someone were urging him on. In the display window were a few pieces of antique furniture: an escritoire with spindly legs, a coat tree with a mirror mounted on it, and a footstool with ratty blue velvet upholstery. Anthony's gaze traveled to the left, and he gasped. He did a double take and then shook his head and laughed. Boy, he really was spooked! In the left-hand corner of the window stood an upholstered rocking chair with a high curved back and tufted arm-rests. An old black overcoat was draped over the back and seat of the chair, and a top hat was held to the coat's collar by a hatpin that had been driven right through the hat's brim and into the cushioned back of the chair. For a split second it had looked as if someone were sitting in the rocker. Anthony laughed again out of sheer relief, and he moved closer to the window. He stood up on tiptoe and peered into the shop to see if he could catch a glimpse of Mr. Magnusson. But he was not there—the shop was lighted but deserted. A creepy feeling began to steal over Anthony, and then he happened to glance to his left again.

His blood froze. There, seated in the rocker, was the pale, withered corpse of Mr. Yurchak. He was dressed in his rumpled blue watchman's uniform, and his glazed unseeing eyes stared straight ahead.

Anthony let out a loud bloodcurdling yell and ran madly down the alley. Pounding in and out of water-filled ruts, he somehow made it out to the street, and he kept on running till he was several blocks away and had to stop because of a horrible pain in his side. Gasping and sobbing, he peered nervously behind him, but no one was following. He took off his red leather cap and wiped his face with a handkerchief. Then he began to shudder all over. It was a convulsive, frightened shudder, and it was some time before he could force it to stop. Finally, when he had pulled himself together, he walked grimly on toward home.

By the time he got to his front door, Anthony was a nervous wreck. He kept looking from side to side, and the shadowy waving of fir boughs in his front yard almost drove him frantic. With a deep sigh of relief, he shut the door behind him and stood dead still for several seconds, listening to his heart beat. From the living room came the friendly chatter of the TV set, and the shower was running upstairs. Reassured by these homey sounds, Anthony started to walk down the hall toward the kitchen, but as he passed the phone it began to ring. When he picked up the receiver, he heard the terrified whispery voice of Miss Eells.

"Anthony? Is that you? Oh, thank God it's you! I was never so happy to hear anyone's voice in my entire life!"

Anthony was stunned, and instantly he forgot about his own fear. "Miss Eells, what's wrong? You sound like you're scared half to death!"

"Well, that's pretty much the way I feel, Anthony!" she answered. "All evening long, someone—or some-*thing*—has been rattling the doors of my house. And that's not all! I saw a face peering in my living room window, and, well, it was like the face of that man you described—you know, the one with the cobwebs on his face? I called the police up an hour ago, but they couldn't find a single sign that anyone had been here. And what's strange is—if anyone had been looking in my living room window he would have been standing in the flower bed. But there weren't any footprints! What on *earth* is going on?"

Anthony was silent for a long time. He swallowed a couple of times before he spoke. "Miss Eells," he said in a weak throaty voice, "I saw something too. Tonight, I mean, on my way home. I don't wanta talk about it on the phone, but . . . well, I think all of this stuff has something to do with that oil lamp. Miss Eells, what are we gonna do?" Fear clutched at Anthony's heart. Had that vision in the antique store window been a warning? Was he going to end up like poor Mr. Yurchak?

This time it was Miss Eells's turn to be silent. Finally, when she spoke, there was the sound of grim determination in her voice. "I think we had better get hold of my brother, Emerson," she said. "If anyone can help us get to the bottom of this weird business, he can."

Anthony smiled. He knew Emerson Eells very well, and he liked him, though he was also a little scared of him. Emerson Eells was a rich lawyer who lived up near St. Cloud, in the central part of Minnesota. He had become an expert on sorcery, and had a whole library of occult books in his home. He also owned several bizarre objects that were supposed to be magic, though he had never been able to demonstrate the powers of any of them. Even so, the little man was a mine of information about pentacles and amulets and demons and spectres and things of that sort.

Anthony and Miss Eells talked a bit more and they both felt a good deal calmer. The next day Miss Eells called Emerson up and told him about all the frightening things that had been going on. He agreed that the lamp must be haunted, and he told Miss Eells not to light it again, for any reason.

"But what do you think we ought to do with it?" she

asked fretfully. "Should I get a hammer and try to smash it?"

"Good heavens, *no!*" exclaimed Emerson. "If you tried to break the lamp, the evil forces inside it would probably strike you dead! Dismantle the thing: Drain out the oil, take out the wick, remove the chimney, and pack the lamp away in a box. Can you put it where it'll be safe and far away from the two of you?"

Miss Eells thought a bit. "Yes. Anthony was using the lamp in a science exhibit. Maybe we could stick it in a locked closet in the chemistry lab where dangerous substances are stored. Anthony could tell Mr. Cardwell, the chemistry teacher, that he was storing the thing there until the science exhibit gets rescheduled."

"Sounds like a good idea," said Emerson. "After you've put the lamp away, I don't want you to do anything. I've got to do some research and some thinking, and then I want you and Anthony to drive up here to St. Cloud so we can have a little conference. By the way, Myra, I really am surprised that it took you so long to figure out that the lamp was causing all the weird goings-on. You have heard of magic lamps, haven't you? Aladdin's lamp, the lamp of Alhazred—these are more than mere fairy tales, and furthermore—"

"Oh, please spare me your wonderful expert knowledge!" exclaimed Miss Eells. "I might have known I'd get lectured when I called on you for help. My problem is that I have a fairly normal mind and I don't make the kinds of weird connections that you do. Have a good time digging through your occult books, and I'll talk to you later."

CHAPTER FIVE

On the following day Miss Eells went down to the library at a very early hour, and she took the lamp apart and packed it into its box and sealed the flaps with masking tape. Then, with shaking hands, she gave the lamp to Anthony, who took it to the chemistry lab at the high school. After he had talked to Mr. Cardwell, the teacher unlocked the heavy oak door of a closet at the back of the lab, and he put the box in a dark corner of the closet, behind a huge glass jug of sulfuric acid. As Mr. Cardwell locked the door, Anthony silently prayed that no more evil things would happen because of the lamp.

Anthony's life went on, in its usual steady routine.

However, an element of fear had been added. Every evening, when he walked home from the library, he felt jittery, and he avoided the street that would take him past Magnusson's Antique Shop. Nothing weird or frightening happened to him, but he began to notice something odd: Mrs. Grimshaw was staring at the library. Once or twice every night he would glance out a window and see her standing under the street lamp on the corner. When he mentioned this to Miss Eells, she smiled knowingly and shook her head.

"I'm not surprised," she said. "I'm not surprised at all. Adele knew perfectly well that she was selling me a haunted lamp, and now she feels guilty about it. Come to think of it, that is probably why she showed up at Mr. Yurchak's funeral. Or maybe it's just a case of morbid curiosity—she's wondering what will happen next. Yuch! What a creep! I don't think I am ever going to visit her wretched shop again. I called her up and tried to find out what she knew about the lamp, but she was very sly and evasive with her answers."

"By the way," said Anthony, changing the subject, "have you heard anything from your brother?"

Miss Eells frowned and shook her head. "Nope," she said, "not a blessed word. Emerson is a very thorough, meticulous sort of person, and sometimes he works *very* slowly. We'll just have to wait."

Two days later, when Anthony went to the library to work after school, he found Miss Eells sitting at the main desk and chewing on a pencil. She was in a very thoughtful mood, and for several minutes she did not seem to be aware that he was standing and staring at her. Then, with a jolt, she broke out of her trance.

"Well . . . er, hello, Anthony, how are you?" said Miss Eells as she glanced about in a flustered way. "Are you going to help me reorganize the card catalog today, or . . . or did you have some other work that has to be done?"

Anthony scowled. "Aw, come on, Miss Eells!" he said grumpily. "Has your brother called you up yet? About the oil lamp and the murder and all that kind of stuff? What did he say? I really want to know."

"No, you don't!" snapped Miss Eells. "If you have any brains in your head, you don't want to know anything about it at all. However, Emerson did call last night, and he thinks we've got a real problem on our hands. He believes that the murder of Mr. Yurchak was only the beginning, and that there'll be worse things to come if we don't do something fast. And so he wants the two of us to come up to his home this weekend so we can figure out what we ought to do. But I warn you, Anthony! Emerson probably has some wild scheme for dealing with the ghost that haunts the oil lamp. He'll try to get the two of us to help him put his plan into action. Whatever you do, don't let him drag you into some lunatic adventure. He's very smart, and very courageous, but he has no right to try to make other people risk their lives. And he can be wrong—oh boy, can he ever be wrong sometimes! But he tries to cover up his ignorance with a smug know-it-all air of . . ."

"Yes? A smug know-it-all air of *what*? Do go on, sister dear. I'm dying to know."

Miss Eells had been doodling on a notepad, but now she looked up. Anthony turned to look too. There, just inside the front door of the library, stood Emerson Eells. He was a short rabbity man with bushy white eyebrows, a well-combed mane of white hair, and large ice-blue eyes that glittered behind gold-rimmed glasses. He was wearing a green tweed jacket and perfectly creased brown tweed trousers. His mouth was curled into an amused smile.

"Well, go on," he said, staring hard at his sister. "What comes next?"

Miss Eells was still totally flabbergasted. "Emerson!" she exclaimed in amazement. "How on earth did you get down here so fast? I just talked to you on the phone last night and . . . why did you come at all? I thought you wanted us to come up and see *you*."

"I changed my mind, Myra," said Emerson smoothly. "May I come in?" Without waiting for an answer, Emerson strode briskly forward and shook Anthony's hand. "Anthony, my boy, how are you? Good Lord, you've grown since I saw you. You must be eating plant food!"

Anthony grinned shyly and muttered something. The

little man was so intelligent, and his eyes shone so brilliantly, that Anthony often had the uncomfortable feeling that Emerson could read his thoughts.

"Now then!" said Emerson, rubbing his hands and glancing around as if he owned the place. "I would like to take the two of you out to dinner so that we can discuss our little problem. Myra, what is the name of that German restaurant on the Wisconsin side of the river? The one that serves the great sauerbraten?"

"It's called Riefschneider's," said Miss Eells. "However," she added dryly, "there is a wee little problem. Anthony and I work at this library, and we're supposed to be here till closing time, at nine o'clock. But maybe I can get hold of Mrs. Willingance. She's a retired librarian, and she subs for me when I'm ill. Hang on a minute."

Miss Eells went to her office to call Mrs. Willingance. She was at home and would be delighted to come in if someone would pick her up.

"Wonderful!" exclaimed Emerson. "If one of you will come along to direct me, I'll zoom over to the dear sweet lady's home and bring her back. Do you know the way, Anthony? Good! Myra, you sit here and think librarial thoughts. We won't be long."

Later that same evening, Miss Eells, Anthony, and Emerson were sitting in a booth in the back of Riefschneider's restaurant. They had eaten their way through a large, heavy meal of sauerbraten, potatoes, and red cabbage, and now they were all quietly sipping coffee. Every so often Miss Eells and Anthony threw expectant glances at Emerson—when was he going to tell them what he knew?

"Oh, come on, Em!" Miss Eells exclaimed when she couldn't stand the suspense any longer. "Did you drag us out here just to make us put on weight? Tell us what you found out!"

Emerson took a last gulp of coffee and reached into the inner pocket of his jacket. He pulled out a yellowed newspaper clipping and, without a word, handed it to his sister. Miss Eells laid the clipping down on the tablecloth between herself and Anthony, and they read it together. The clipping was from the Minneapolis *Tribune*, and it was dated March 12, 1931. The large black headline over the article said STRANGE SCARECROW BURIAL IN WISCONSIN TOWN, and beneath this heading a rather odd tale was told:

> *Stillwater, Wisconsin.* Last Friday the elderly and eccentric lawyer Willis Nightwood died at his house outside this tiny town in northern Wisconsin. Two days later Mr. Nightwood's body was cremated, and on the day after the cremation, a bizarre burial took place. This mock funeral was performed according to instructions left in the old lawyer's will: A

scarecrow dressed in Mr. Nightwood's black overcoat was placed in an open coffin. It was then taken to an underground room that had been constructed during Mr. Nightwood's lifetime. The room is solidly built of bricks and mortar, and lies thirty feet underground beneath a hill on Mr. Nightwood's property. After some occult ceremonies were performed, the scarecrow was carried down a long sloping ramp to the brick room and was then taken from its coffin and propped up in a sitting position in a chair. Next, the chair was pulled up to an oak table on which three things had been placed: a large family Bible, a small hand bell, and a Dutch china oil lamp that had been Mr. Nightwood's bedside lamp for years. Finally, the room was sealed: Two heavy iron inner doors were locked, and the ramp leading to the room was blocked with earth and boulders. When all this had been done, the entrance at the top of the ramp was filled with three feet of freshly poured concrete, and when the concrete had hardened, a brass plaque with the words IT TAKES JACKS TO OPEN was fastened to the smooth surface of the concrete. This mysterious message probably refers to Mr. Nightwood's poker-playing days. It is well known in Stillwater that he made a great deal of money from poker when he was a young

man, though no one can figure out why he
would want to put a poker-playing inscription
on the grotesque "tomb" he constructed. Some
have suggested that the inscription may be a
riddle or code of some sort, but if it is . . .

At this point the article ended. The scrap of paper
had been snipped out of a newspaper page, but part of
the story was missing. Miss Eells glared indignantly at
her brother.

"Well? Where's the rest of it?" she asked.

Emerson shrugged. "It's all I could find," he said. "This
clipping was in a scrapbook that I found in the Reference Room of the St. Cloud Public Library. It seems
that, over the years, the librarians there have kept a series of scrapbooks about odd things that have happened
in Minnesota and Wisconsin. I used my influence and
asked one of the nice ladies if I might borrow the clipping for a little bit. I got to talking with the lady about
the Nightwood case, and she told me about something
that happened on July ninth of this year. So I went
down to the room where the old newspapers are kept,
and I found the article that I wanted. This time I didn't
ask for permission—I merely ripped the piece out of the
paper." Emerson smiled and reached into his jacket
pocket. He pulled out a ragged piece of newspaper that
was much whiter and cleaner than the other one.

"I hope no one will mind that I damaged the library's

newspaper to get this," he said as he laid the article on the table. "But I felt that my thievery was being done for a good cause."

"I always knew you had the makings of a vandal in you," said Miss Eells, grinning. "Well now, let's see what *this* one has to say!"

With their heads close together, Miss Eells and Anthony read the second article, which was also from the Minneapolis *Tribune*. It said:

WEIRD BREAK-IN ON NIGHTWOOD ESTATE

Stillwater, Wisconsin. Last night some unknown person or persons tunneled into the hill that contains the famous scarecrow "tomb" of the old Nightwood estate. Mr. Jake Swiggert, the present owner of the estate, said that he discovered the break-in early this morning when he was taking a walk. By crawling into the tunnel, Mr. Swiggert found that a portion of the brick wall of the underground vault had been knocked down, and the room had been entered. The place was in total disarray: The scarecrow had been knocked from its chair and the oak table had been overturned, but the only thing missing from the tomb chamber was the small Dutch china oil lamp that had been placed on the table when the tomb was sealed. When asked why he thought thieves would

want to enter the tomb, Mr. Swiggert said that
they were probably looking for treasure. It is
true that rumors have circulated for many years
about the gold and jewels and other valuables
that were supposedly concealed in the mysterious underground vault, but Mr. Swiggert is convinced that nothing of any value was taken—
except, of course, the oil lamp. Mr. Swiggert
says that he intends to have the hole filled in
and the bricks replaced in the wall of the room,
but he will take no further precautions.

"Hey!" said Anthony, looking up suddenly. "So *that's*
how old Mrs. Whosis got hold of that lamp! She must've
bought it from the creep that broke into the tomb."

"Exactly," said Emerson smoothly. "And then Mrs.
Grimshaw found out that she had a haunted oil lamp
on her hands, and she decided to unload it on dear old
Myra here. Myra has many good qualities, but she's a
bit gullible, and loves antiques. Mrs. Grimshaw must
have realized that she would be an easy mark."

"Thanks a whole lot, Em!" said Miss Eells sourly.
"But now that you've finished handing out the compli-
ments, let me ask you something. *We've* got the lamp
now, and it has already killed one person and may kill
more. Furthermore, it has frightened Anthony and me
half to death, and yet you say that it would not be a
good idea to try and destroy it. All right! *Then what in
the name of all that's holy are we going to do?*"

Emerson paused. He reached into his jacket pocket and pulled out a meerschaum pipe with a bowl shaped like a turbaned head. As Anthony and Miss Eells watched in exasperated silence, he picked up a small leather pouch that lay on the table and used it to fill his pipe. Finally he spoke.

"I like dramatic pauses," he explained as he puffed. "But to get back to your question: We should take the oil lamp up to Stillwater and put it back in the underground room, where it belongs. Did either of you notice the significance of the three objects that were on the table in that room?"

"Hmm . . ." muttered Miss Eells, as she began counting the objects on her fingers, "Bible, hand bell, oil lamp . . . hey! That's almost like bell, book, and candle, isn't it?"

Emerson smiled mockingly and clapped his hands. "Bravo! Your college education was not wasted after all, Myra! Bell, book, and candle were used in one of the rites of exorcism: When people wanted to get rid of an evil spirit, they rang the bell to frighten it away, then they closed the Bible to shut the spirit out of the world of God-fearing people, and lastly, they blew out the candle to extinguish the spirit's light and send it back into the black pit of Hell." Emerson paused again and puffed at his pipe. "I think," he went on, "that Willis Nightwood was possessed by an evil spirit. How this happened I don't know—maybe he was practicing black magic in secret, and he did something very foolish and got possessed. . . . I just don't know. Anyway, I think there was a good side to old Nightwood, a sane side that didn't want the evil spirit wandering around after he was dead. So he enchanted the bell, the book, and the lamp, and arranged them in a certain way on that table in the underground room that he built. Maybe he worked some hocus-pocus with that scarecrow too . . . who knows? So far, so good! The evil spirit is trapped in the dark chamber, trapped forever . . . but not *quite* forever. When that idiot tunneled into the tomb, he broke the spell, and now the haunted lamp is out in the world, and wherever it goes, the spirit goes, and it takes on the shape of Willis Nightwood and it does horrible things. So we have got to put it back before more damage is done!"

Anthony stared at Emerson. "You mean you're gonna go up to that little town in Wisconsin and ask Mr. Whatsisname to let you put the lamp back into the room?"

Emerson rolled his eyes upward and laughed. "Oh dear, no! If I tried to do that, good old Mr. Swiggert would decide that I had rocks in my head, and he would either call the police or the local insane asylum. No, I'm afraid we're going to have to go sneaking at night, tippy-toe, and burrow into that hill just the way the burglar did. It won't be much fun, and it'll probably be danger-ous, but we simply can't leave things the way they are. That lamp is—"

"I beg your pardon, brother dear," said Miss Eells, interrupting, "but would you kindly tell me who you mean by *we*? Were you expecting the two of us to help you carry out this harebrained scheme?"

Emerson looked offended. "It is *not* a harebrained scheme, and to answer your question, yes, I was ex-pecting you to help me, Myra. But I wouldn't dream of dragging Anthony into this."

"Just try and keep me out of it," muttered Anthony through clenched teeth.

"What did you say?" said Emerson, blinking.

Miss Eells glanced quickly at Anthony, and then she folded her arms and wrinkled her nose skeptically. "Em," she said slowly, "I don't mean to be a wet blanket, but there are still a lot of loose ends to this wonderful plan of yours. What if we get up to Stillwater and find that Mr. Swiggert has made it impossible for us to get into that underground room? I know he said he was just going to fill in the hole, but what if he changed his mind? What if we go up there and find that he has put up an electrified barbed-wire fence and has turned loose a pack of German shepherd dogs to guard his property? Then what? I think we ought to check the situation out before we go charging up to Stillwater with that cursed rotten oil lamp."

Emerson stiffened. He did not like it when people criticized his wonderful plans. "Yes, Myra," he said in a biting tone. "You're saying that we should sit around and do nothing while that evil vampirish thing is on the loose. Do you want Anthony to be his next victim? Or would you prefer it to be yourself? Or me?"

Miss Eells glared at her brother. Her face was getting red, and it was clear that she was struggling to keep from losing her temper. "I don't want *anyone* to get hurt, Em," she said in a strained voice, "and that is why I think we ought to go slow. Besides, I think we will be safe for the time being. After all, you're the one who told us what to do with the lamp, and you were right—nothing has happened since we locked it up, and so I think we ought to just leave the dratted thing in the chemistry lab until we find out if it's really possible for us to stick it back into that tomb where it belongs. Doesn't that make sense to you?"

Emerson smiled thoughtfully. "We-ell, I *suppose* so," he said slowly, "but I think you're missing something important."

Miss Eells's eyes flashed. "Oh?" she said sharply. "And what is that, pray tell?"

"You've got your sleeve in the sauerbraten sauce."

CHAPTER SIX

Half a week dragged past. Each day after school Anthony raced off to the library to find out if Miss Eells had any news. But each time that Anthony asked, Miss Eells said that she hadn't heard a thing from Emerson, who had driven up to Stillwater to check out Mr. Swiggert's farm. Nothing, not a peep, not even so much as a phone call. However, she said that she was not ready to push the panic button yet. Emerson was a strange and infuriating person, and he liked to keep people waiting until he was ready to give them his exciting news.

Finally, on Friday evening, Emerson returned. He was cheerful and fairly bubbling over with enthusiasm because he had found out that the mound was practically unguarded. There was no electric fence, there were no grinning guard dogs. Breaking in would be a cinch, an absolute pushover!

Miss Eells sat in her office, listening to her brother's breathless report. Emerson was perched on a stool near the desk, and Anthony was sitting in an armchair in a corner. It was nine-thirty, and the library had been closed for half an hour. One would have thought that Miss Eells would be overjoyed to hear what Emerson had to say. But instead she seemed puzzled and upset.

"Em," she said at last, when he had paused to catch his breath, "I'm a little bit confused. You say that there aren't any problems about getting into the tomb. The place is just wide open, waiting for us to go up and burrow into the hill and put the lamp back where it belongs. But if everything is so wonderful and hunky-dory, why did you stay up in Stillwater for three days?"

Emerson grimaced. "I didn't have much choice in the matter, sister dear. My car burned out a bearing and I had to wait until the guy at the local garage could order the part and have it installed. But now I think we are ready to get moving. Anthony, do you think you could get your science teacher to unlock his lab so we can get the lamp tomorrow morning? I know it's a Saturday, but maybe you could make up some reason for—"

"I think it'll be okay," said Anthony, interrupting. "Mr. Cardwell usually works there on Saturdays. He feeds the lab animals and messes around with experiments. I'll call him up tomorrow morning and see if he'll let us in."

Early on Saturday morning, Miss Eells, Emerson, and Anthony were standing outside one of the side doors of Hoosac High School. Through the glass panels, they saw a tall lean man with a leathery, tanned face. He held a ring of keys and he looked rather puzzled, but he smiled politely as he opened the door.

"I hope we're not causing you a lot of trouble, Mr. Cardwell," said Miss Eells as she walked past him. "But I'm sure Anthony must have told you that I do need the lamp that you've been keeping for him. We're having an antiques exhibit at the library on Monday, and Mrs. Oxenstern will have a fit if everything isn't just so when the exhibit opens."

Mr. Cardwell winced. He was well acquainted with the bossy woman who was the head of the Library Board. "I get you, Miss Eells," he said with a grim little chuckle.

The visitors followed Mr. Cardwell to the chemistry lab. Out came the key ring again, and the teacher unlocked the closet door, which creaked as he pulled it open.

"I'll get it for you," said Mr. Cardwell as he stepped into the closet. "It ought to be right behind that big jug of . . ." His voice trailed away as he stopped dead in his tracks. Quickly Anthony peered over the teacher's shoulder into the dark corner where he had put the box that held the lamp. But the box was gone.

Anthony stepped back into the room and threw a frightened glance at Emerson and Miss Eells. Meanwhile Mr. Cardwell anxiously moved jars and bottles around. There was a long tense silence while Mr. Cardwell searched, until finally he heaved a disheartened sigh and turned to face his visitors. He looked very embarrassed and unhappy.

"I'll be darned if *I* know what happened to the thing!" Mr. Cardwell muttered as he shook his head. "I remember very well seeing Anthony put that box in behind the sulfuric acid jug. And nobody has a key to this closet except me. How on earth could—"

Mr. Cardwell's hand flew to his mouth. A thought had just occurred to him. Turning, he walked to the back of the closet and stared up at a ladder that was bolted to the wall. Anthony had seen the ladder before, but he hadn't thought about it much. Now, as he watched, Mr. Cardwell put his foot on one of the lower rungs and started to climb. When he reached the ceiling he raised his fist and thumped at a panel of wood that was set in the ceiling. Then he pushed and the panel flew back. Daylight flooded into the closet.

"Hah! I *thought* so!" growled Mr. Cardwell. "This trapdoor should be hooked from the inside, but it isn't. Somebody got up onto the roof of the school and came in this way to steal the lamp. Pretty darned clever!"

Miss Eells turned pale and she grabbed at Emerson's arm. Anthony knew what they were thinking: The lamp wasn't very valuable in itself. No one would go to the trouble of stealing it unless he knew that the lamp was magic.

Gently Emerson pried his sister's fingers loose from his arm. Then he took off his jacket and handed it to her. "Here, sis," he said. "Hold this for me while I go have a quick scamper across the roof of this noble institution." He turned and glanced quickly at Mr. Cardwell. "You don't have any objections, I hope?"

Mr. Cardwell shook his head. "Nope. Go right ahead."

As the others watched, Emerson climbed nimbly up the ladder and wriggled out through the trapdoor hole. Five minutes passed until Emerson reappeared. Humming quietly to himself, he climbed back into the room and took his jacket from Miss Eells.

"Did you find anything?" asked Anthony anxiously.

"Not a great deal," muttered Emerson as he put his jacket back on. "There's a loose trapdoor over on the other side of the roof. I lifted it and peered in—seems to be a storeroom of some kind. You really ought to speak to the janitor, Mr. Cardwell. This business of leaving trapdoors unhooked all over the place . . . it's not a good idea."

Mr. Cardwell scowled. "It hasn't been a problem until now," he said. "I mean, we have never had a break-in at Hoosac High before. And I'll be darned if I can see why this one happened. Was that lamp really worth a lot of dough?"

Miss Eells gave Emerson an odd look, and then she forced a smile. "Fortunately, no, it isn't very, uh, valuable," she said, hemming and hawing a bit. "But it . . . er, it had a good deal of, um, sentimental value to me. You know how these things are."

Mr. Cardwell stared at Miss Eells curiously. "Sentimental value?" he said in a wondering tone. "Anthony told me that you bought the thing down in Dresbach just a little while ago. How could you get sentimental about it in that length of time?"

Miss Eells's face was getting red. "Well, uh, did I use the word *sentimental*?" she asked, waving her hand in a flustered way. "How foolish of me! I meant that it, uh, had a good deal of, uh, charm value. Yes, that's what I meant to say—it was utterly charming, what with that Dutch china base and all those cute little, uh, Dutch pictures. You know what I mean?"

"My sister is not always terribly precise in her speech," said Emerson dryly. "But to return to important matters: As far as I can tell, the only people who knew that the lamp was in here are the four of us. Isn't that so, Myra?"

Miss Eells nodded. "I suppose so. I certainly didn't tell anybody else. Did you, Anthony?"

"Nope. I don't think I even told my mom or dad or my brother, Keith, about it. I wonder who swiped it?"

Miss Eells thanked the chemistry teacher for being so patient, and then the three visitors left. When they were back inside Emerson's car, Miss Eells let out a string of very fancy swear words. She was angry and frightened and very frustrated.

"I know how you feel, Myra," said Emerson as he lit his meerschaum pipe. "This is a very puzzling business. The bloody lamp is haunted, and I cannot for the life of me see why anyone would want to take it. I mean, it would be like stealing a poisonous plant, or a chunk of radioactive material. Of course, the ghost might have stolen it, but then why didn't he do it earlier, when the lamp was in Mrs. Grimshaw's shop? Actually, if the ghost really did take it—which I doubt—he wouldn't have needed to pop in through a trapdoor, would he? I *still* do not see what good the lamp would do to the ghost or *anybody*! That is the thing that is really driving me crazy: *Why* was the lamp stolen?"

"Maybe we have a mad lamp collector in our midst," said Miss Eells with a grim chuckle. She paused and scratched her chin. "I have to admit that the whole business has me stumped," she went on. "But I do think we can be certain about one thing: If the thief is fool enough to light the lamp, he'll be very sorry. And we'll be reading about another ghastly murder in the news-papers."

"I wish I thought that the thief was a fool who didn't know about the powers of the lamp," said Emerson as he puffed his pipe meditatively. "If I thought that, I wouldn't be so nervous. But I have the horrible feeling that the thief is a very clever person who knows a lot more than we do."

"What do you think the thief knows?" asked Anthony anxiously.

Emerson shrugged helplessly and said nothing.

After a few days Emerson went back up to St. Cloud, and Miss Eells and Anthony returned to their normal everyday routine. Winter plodded on, with wintry gales and a heavy snowfall. Every day, when he went out to get the morning paper, Anthony expected to read about a murder that was somehow connected with a haunted oil lamp. But the deaths were the usual ones, reported in the picturesque style of the Hoosac *Daily Sentinel*: If somebody important died, the *Sentinel* would have a short article with a heading like MRS. ETHEL ODEGARD SUC-CUMBS, or DEATH CLAIMS T. R. CREECH. But there were no articles about bodies turned to withered papery husks. No magic lamps had been seen hovering through the mists along the Mississippi River. Nevertheless, the mystery of the lamp stayed on Anthony's mind, and on Miss Eells's mind too. To make themselves feel better, they tried to find out as much as they could about Willis Nightwood, the sinister old man who had built the scarecrow's "tomb" up in Stillwater, Wisconsin. But there wasn't an awful lot to find out: Willis Nightwood had not been famous, he had just been weird, and there weren't any books about him. Miss Eells phoned the public library in Stillwater, and the librarian sent her a copy of the article that had appeared in the local paper on the day Mr. Nightwood died. From this article Miss Eells found out a few things that she hadn't known before: She learned that Mr. Nightwood had built a large elaborate summer home on an island in Stillwater Lake; and she also learned that he had left a large collection of legal books, which were sold by his relatives. Some of these books had wound up in the public library in Hoosac, where Anthony and Miss Eells worked.

"It's not much to go on," said Miss Eells after she told Anthony what she had found out. "But I suppose it's better than nothing. The next time you have a few spare moments, go to the legal section in the stacks and see if you can find any books with a bookplate or a signature that says Willis Nightwood."

Anthony looked blank. "What do I do then?"

Miss Eells smiled mischievously. "Why, bring them to my office. Then, after everyone has gone home, we will go over these books with a fine-tooth comb. We will rip the pages loose from the bindings and tear apart the covers to see if anything is sewn up inside. I'm a librarian, and I don't much like destroying books, but if I can find one little teeny-tiny clue that will help us solve the mystery we have on our hands, it will be worth it."

That evening, after the library closed, Anthony came to Miss Eells's office with three dusty volumes bound in black pebble-grained leather. Each one had a bookplate pasted on the inside part of the front cover, and the bookplates all said EX LIBRIS WILLIS NIGHTWOOD. As Anthony watched, Miss Eells solemnly shook each volume, but nothing fell out, not even a dead moth. Then she took a penknife and sliced through the spine of each book. She ripped the moldy leather away from the stiff cardboard covers of the books and peered till her eyes were sore, but she found nothing—absolutely nothing.

A week passed. On a snowy night in December, Anthony and his family were sitting in the living room in front of the television set. They were watching *The Jackie Gleason Show*, a program that Anthony loved: He was always running around the house imitating Jackie's struts and sayings, like *Aaaand a-wayyyy we GO!* So he was a bit irritated when the phone rang just as Reggie Van Gleason III was going into one of his routines.

"Can you get it, Ma?" he asked grumpily. "I really wanta watch this."

"So do I!" his mother shot back. "And if I remember correctly, I answered the phone three times during television shows last night, and each time it was for you."

"We oughta just take the phone off the hook durin' this show," growled Keith, Anthony's older brother. "Will one of you go get it? Come on!"

Meanwhile, the phone went on ringing. At last, wearily, Anthony pushed himself to his feet and stumbled out into the dining room, where the phone was. He pulled the sliding door shut and picked up the receiver. It was Miss Eells, and she was really in a state.

"Anthony? Hello, is that you? Oh, good! I was so afraid that you'd be out! Listen, I just got the strangest phone call from Adele Grimshaw. She called to tell me that she had some information about the lamp, and she wants me to come out to her place."

"Why didn't she just tell you over the phone?" asked Anthony.

"I suggested that, but she wouldn't hear of it. Anthony, you have no idea how nervous that woman was! She was practically crawling out of her skin, and half the time she didn't sound like herself at all! She was really *upset*!" Miss Eells paused and sighed. "Of course I will admit," she went on, "that this so-called 'information' may be something that Adele dreamed up on her own. But I feel that I have to go. I wonder if you'd care to ride along with me."

Anthony stifled a groan. Tomorrow was Sunday, and in the morning he was planning to play basketball with Ted Hoopenbecker and some other boys down at the high school gym. But the mysterious disappearing lamp had been on his mind a lot, and if Mrs. Grimshaw had any news about it, he wanted to know. Besides, he was afraid of letting Miss Eells go into a dangerous situation by herself. For all he knew, the lamp thief might be

lurking around out at Mrs. Grimshaw's place. If anything bad happened to Miss Eells, Anthony would never
forgive himself.

"Okay, I'll come," he said after a long pause. "What
time do you want to pick me up?"

It was a bright, clear, wintry morning when Miss Eells
and Anthony started off toward Dresbach. Snow glittered on the high bluffs above the Mississippi, and river
barges hooted as their car rolled past. On the way, Miss
Eells talked a blue streak. She babbled about everything
under the sun—her feud with Mrs. Oxenstern, the price
of Royal Doulton china, and the trouble she was having
with the kids who threw spit wads in the East Reading
Room. Anthony could not get a word in edgewise. He
knew Miss Eells pretty well, and he knew that she was
extremely nervous. Finally, when she had paused to catch
her breath, he spoke.

"Miss Eells? What're you so antsy about? Do you think
goin' to see that woman is gonna be dangerous?"

Miss Eells looked startled, and then she laughed. "You
are getting to be a very perceptive young man! If you
really want to know, I'm *very* nervous about this trip. I
didn't like the way Adele sounded over the phone, and
I really can't imagine what she has to tell me. But when
we get there, try to act calm or she'll have a conniption
right before our eyes. Let me do the talking. Okay?"

Anthony nodded.

When they arrived in Dresbach, they cruised through the tiny downtown section, and then turned off onto a steep side street that led to Mrs. Grimshaw's antique shop. Over the bare trees rose the cupola of the fancy old Victorian house. Miss Eells nosed her car into the parking lot and shut off the motor. When they opened the door, they saw that there was no one in either of the two big downstairs rooms. The house was silent, and a strong smell of burning kerosene hung in the air.

"Hello, Adele!" Miss Eells called when she reached the bottom of the main staircase. "Are you home?"

No answer.

"She's probably in her office in the back," muttered Miss Eells. "Come on."

Anthony followed Miss Eells down a narrow back hall to a paneled door that stood slightly ajar. Peering in, Anthony saw a tiny room that held a rolltop desk littered with bills and other papers. A floor lamp stood nearby, and beyond it was a set of shelves built into the far wall: The shelves held broken mechanical antiques— cast-iron banks, clocks, and a couple of music boxes. Pulled up to the desk was a swivel chair, and in it sat something that made Anthony's eyes open wide. At first he thought it was a white plaster statue, a statue dressed in Mrs. Grimshaw's clothes and fitted with a wig that looked like Mrs. Grimshaw's hair. The figure was hunched over the desk and it gripped a pen in its chalky fingers. As Anthony and Miss Eells watched in frozen horror, the strange shape turned and stared at them, and they saw that living human eyes burned in its head. The pale mouth opened, and then the figure dissolved. It fell to pieces before their eyes, and there was nothing left but a sagging empty dress and a whitish powder that ran out across the floor and then lay in a whispering, drifting heap at their feet.

CHAPTER SEVEN

Miss Eells and Anthony stood in the doorway for a long time. They stared at the limp dress that lay draped across the desk. The strange dust moved about in snaky trails and then lay still. Suddenly, with a little yelp, Miss Eells turned and dashed out into the hall. She stood there with her hands clasped over her face, and she shuddered convulsively. Anthony didn't move. He felt stunned, and he kept thinking: It got her—the ghost got her. It killed her the way it killed Mr. Yurchak. He didn't for a minute think that the white figure in the chair was a statue—he was utterly convinced that it was Mrs. Grimshaw, changed by the evil magic of the ghost that haunted the lamp.

Miss Eells took her hands away from her face. She looked pale and frightened, but she also looked determined. Seizing Anthony by the arm, she pulled him out into the hall.

"Come on!" she said, tugging anxiously. "We've got to get out of here! If anyone shows up, we'll have a lot of explaining to do, and people may even get the crazy idea that *we* did away with Mrs. Grimshaw. Come on, Anthony! I know it's awful, but we can't do any good here. We've got to go!"

Stumbling along like a sleepwalker, Anthony followed Miss Eells to the car. After fumbling for a long time in her handbag, Miss Eells found her car keys, and she started the motor. Off they drove, and for a long time neither said anything. Finally Anthony broke the silence.

"Do . . . do you really think anybody will figure out that the powder on the floor is . . . is . . ."

"Is really all that's left of Adele?" Miss Eells cut in with a grimace. "I don't know. I really, truly couldn't say. Policemen aren't very imaginative, but they may eventually decide that Adele is gone. Oh, Lord! What a horrible way to go! And you know, the way things look now, Adele is the one who stole the lamp."

"It kind of looks that way," muttered Anthony.

"And now that I think about it," Miss Eells went on, pursing up her lips, "I must have tipped her off about the lamp's hiding place when I talked to her on the phone the other day. So she must have stolen it. But why on *earth* would she want to do a stupid thing like that? She sold it to me to get rid of it, because she knew it was haunted. So why would she want it back? This whole thing makes absolutely no sense at all! Can *you* figure it out?"

Anthony shook his head, and they drove in silence to Hoosac.

For the next two days Miss Eells and Anthony combed the newspapers and listened to local radio stations, hoping to hear some news of Mrs. Grimshaw. Finally, on the third day, they saw an article in the Hoosac *Sentinel* about the mysterious disappearance of Mrs. Grimshaw. Her store had been found empty, and the rooms upstairs where she lived did not show any sign of a struggle. There was no mention of a white powder, or any empty dress draped across Mrs. Grimshaw's desk.

"What do you think happened to that powder?" asked Anthony, who was reading the article over Miss Eells's shoulder.

Miss Eells shrugged. "Search me! And if you think the disappearing powder is odd, here's something even odder: 'Police revealed that, shortly before her disappearance, Mrs. Grimshaw withdrew all her money from the La Crosse Savings Bank. The amount was in excess of $200,000.' " Miss Eells looked up at Anthony. "Now tell me, my friend, why the dickens did she do *that*?

You can hardly say that the ghost made her do it, because ghosts don't need money—at least, I never heard of one that did. There's something very fishy here. Do you have any bright ideas?"

Anthony said that he was stumped, and after a long discussion the two of them realized that they were just going around in circles. So they tried to forget about the whole frightening business, but they found that they couldn't. And they both got that creepy feeling that people get when they are waiting for something to happen.

Needless to say, Miss Eells called up her brother, Emerson, but he did not have any wonderful advice to offer. *Wait and see if something else happens* was what he kept saying, but this did not satisfy Miss Eells. And as the days of December passed, she became more and more convinced that waiting was no good.

On the day after Christmas, Anthony went over to Miss Eells's house to see how she was getting along. School was out and he had a lot of time on his hands, and besides, he really wanted to talk to her. Sad to say, Anthony never enjoyed talking to anyone in his family as much as he did Miss Eells, who he felt was the only person in the world who really understood him. When he got to her house, he rang her door bell and then stood on the front stoop for a long time, jingling the change in his pocket. Where was she, anyway? Suddenly Anthony heard a muffled swishing and clinking, and some loud noises that sounded like swearing. Then he heard footsteps, and Miss Eells opened the door. Her face was red, and in one hand she clutched a broken pine bough and a clump of tinsel icicles. In her hair were more icicles and some pine needles.

"The tree fell over," she announced in solemn tones. Then—quite unexpectedly—she laughed. Anthony was relieved at this. Together the two of them managed to get the Christmas tree back into an upright position, and Anthony fiddled with the legs of the metal standard, which was tippy and totally unreliable. He was a pretty handy young man, and he steadied the tree and tightened the screws that held it in place, while Miss Eells gathered up the broken ornaments and put them into a paper bag. Finally, when the living room was all tidied up, the two of them went to the kitchen to get something to eat. Miss Eells set out a plate of fancy Christmas cookies and candies, and she poured each of them a glass of milk.

"Cheers," said Miss Eells as she raised her glass. Then she added, unexpectedly, "I'm driving up to Stillwater the day after tomorrow. Would you care to come along?"

Anthony's mouth dropped open, and he nearly spilled his milk.

Miss Eells grinned mischievously. "Surprised you, didn't I? Well, this little decision has been coming on for some time now. I've thought about my dear brother's advice, and I've come to the conclusion that waiting is about as sensible as smoking in a room full of gunpowder. A lot of very odd things have been going on lately, and nothing makes sense. I know that supernatural events aren't supposed to be sensible, but I can't shake off the feeling that there's going to be trouble soon. So I'm going to motor up to good old Mr. Nightwood's hometown to see what I can find out. If there's an answer to this oil lamp mystery, I am convinced it's up there."

Anthony munched his cookie and looked thoughtful. He did not care much for Miss Eells's plan. He was afraid—afraid of what they might find. They might walk in on something they couldn't handle.

Miss Eells was watching Anthony. She popped a chocolate cream into her mouth and chewed it slowly. "You think my little plan is lousy, don't you?" she said with a sour grimace.

Anthony felt embarrassed. He stared at the tablecloth and frowned. "Uh, well . . ." he began nervously, "it's just that, uh, I was kind of wondering what we'd do if we ran into something really awful. Like that ghost, the one that killed Mrs. Grimshaw and Mr. Yurchak."

"We'd give him the high hard one over the outside corner," said Miss Eells calmly. "It's well-known that ghosts can't hit a high fast ball. But to be a little more serious, I think you've got a good point: What *could* we do, if that cobweb-faced ghoul came after us? On the other hand, if we're clever and observant, we might get there in time to stop something dreadful from happening. You see, Anthony, that is the idea I can't get out of my mind: I keep thinking that a forty-ton safe is going to drop on us from above. It's up there, hanging by a thread, right now. Am I making any sense to you?"

Anthony didn't want to answer. He broke a piece of peanut brittle in two and chewed part of it noisily. "Why do you want me to come along?" he asked as he munched.

Miss Eells looked ashamed. She sighed. "I want you to come because I'm scared of going alone," she said in a low voice. "I've asked Emerson to come, but—like you—he thinks my ideas are totally stupid. As far as he's concerned, the ghost and the lamp have vanished back into the black pit and they'll never be heard from again. I'm afraid to go alone, but I know very well that I'll regret it if I don't go." She paused and stared dejectedly at the floor. "You don't have to come if you don't want to," she muttered.

Anthony didn't know what to say. Miss Eells was his best friend in all the world, and he didn't want anything bad to happen to her. On the other hand, he didn't feel like following her into a quicksand bog. He stared out the window at the dead weeds that poked up through the snow in Miss Eells's backyard. Anthony knew this eccentric old lady pretty well. If she got an idea into her head, nobody could make her change her mind. She would go up to Stillwater by herself if she had to, and then . . . If she was killed or injured, Anthony would feel guilty for the rest of his life.

"Oh, *okay*!" sighed Anthony wearily. "I'll go with you. But if that cobwebby thing comes after us, I don't know what *I* can do!"

So it was decided: They would go up to Stillwater two days later. Anthony didn't have any trouble getting permission from his mother—she was tired of seeing him moping about the house during the school vacation. Miss Eells thought about telling Emerson what they were doing, but she decided that he would just worry, so she said nothing.

Off they went. They drove for three hours straight until they came to Stillwater. It was a typical small midwestern town with a main street three blocks long and lots of big old wooden houses. The town hall was four stories high, and it was made of red brick. It had a clock tower with a greenish copper roof and a huge arched entrance flanked by polished granite columns. Miss Eells nosed her battered old Dodge into a parking place in front of this impressive building. With a sigh of relief she turned the motor off.

"Well, Anthony, this is it!" said Miss Eells, leaning back in her seat and folding her arms. She smiled contentedly. "Don't you just love small towns?"

Anthony's heart sank. On the way up he had been nervous and afraid, but now that he had actually seen this dreary little burg, he wanted to leave. Stillwater reminded him of a town in Minnesota called Blue Pigeon, where two of this mother's most horrible relatives, Aunt Elda and Uncle Hartley, lived. It was hard for Anthony to believe anything dangerous or exciting would happen to them while they were here.

Miss Eells glanced at Anthony, and she read his thoughts. But she said nothing. Instead she picked up her purse, got out of the car, and started walking toward the front door of the town hall. Anthony sprang quickly out of the car and followed her. He felt vaguely alarmed, and he wondered what she was up to.

"Miss Eells?" he asked as they walked along. "Whatcha doin'?"

She smiled calmly. "I'm going in to see if the folks here have any folders about the town's history and its old buildings. We might find out something new about the scarecrow tomb, or that summer home that Nightwood built out on an island in Stillwater Lake. We have to start somewhere."

Anthony and Miss Eells walked in through the swinging glass doors, and they found that they were in a high-ceilinged entrance hall that ran all the way to the other end of the building. Doors with frosted-glass panes opened off the hall, and the walls were covered with gloomy, dusty murals that had been sketched out on the walls when the plaster was still wet. Anthony saw battle scenes, explorers canoeing on the Mississippi, and various landscapes.

"Good gravy!" exclaimed Miss Eells as she glanced around. "Get a load of these wall paintings, will you? Who on earth do you suppose painted them? The style isn't bad, is it?"

Anthony shrugged. He always got embarrassed when Miss Eells asked him for opinions on subjects he didn't know anything about. "I guess they're all right," he muttered as he moved closer to the wall. Suddenly he stopped and stared, and he motioned for Miss Eells to come over to where he was standing. "Hey, look!" he exclaimed. "This is a funny kind of picture. What do you think it's supposed to mean?"

Miss Eells stepped up to the wall and squinted. The light was not too good, but she saw what Anthony was staring at. In the middle of the landscapes the painter had put in a view of the inside of a room. A rather odd room. Against one wall stood something that looked like an altar, and on the altar squatted a red statue of a woman who wore a golden crown on her head and held a sceptre in her right hand. Her left hand pointed toward her forehead, and there were letters there, though they were too small to read. Two niches were cut in the wall above the altar, and they held statues. Light streamed into the room from an oval window set high up on one of the side walls, and it fell on a low circular pedestal that stood in the middle of the floor. On the pedestal stood something small and somehow familiar—at least, it seemed familiar to Anthony and Miss Eells. It looked like an oil lamp.

CHAPTER EIGHT

For a long time Miss Eells and Anthony stood there, staring at the painting in silence. They both felt cold and a little queasy. What did this picture mean? Why was it here? It didn't fit in with any of the other scenes on the nearby walls. Suddenly Miss Eells stepped forward. She took a handkerchief out of her purse, spat on it a couple of times, and rubbed at a dusty patch on the wall. There, at the bottom of the painting of the strange room, was a name: *Willis Nightwood*. Nearby the date *1929* had been scrawled in black paint.

With a satisfied grunt, Miss Eells stuffed her handkerchief back into her purse and turned away. "Well, Anthony!" she said in a voice that trembled a little. "We seem to have discovered something new about our batty old friend, Mr. Nightwood. But it's hard to tell what that painting means—if, indeed, it means anything at all. What do you think?"

Anthony shook his head. "I dunno, Miss Eells. I wish I knew what that picture was for. Do you think maybe there's a room somewhere that looks like that?"

Miss Eells was about to say something, but she stepped sideways and bumped into an American flag that was standing in a metal holder. The flagpole rocked dangerously, and then it fell over with a loud clatter that echoed in the high ceiling. As Miss Eells and Anthony struggled to get the tall, heavy flagpole back into an upright position again, one of the nearby doors opened, and a woman stepped in. She was about sixty years old, with a saggy, friendly face and a bun of gray hair. A pencil was stuck in her hair, and black straps hung down from her horn-rimmed glasses. As soon as the woman saw what had happened, she laughed.

"Lord above!" she exclaimed. "I thought somebody had been shot! Well, you two sure get the clumsiness prize. Here, let me help you."

Miss Eells knew she was clumsy, but she hated to be reminded of the fact. After the three of them managed to shove the flag back into place, the woman wiped her hands on her skirt and introduced herself: She was Inez Bracegirdle, the town clerk.

"And what brings you folks up here to our fair city?" Mrs. Bracegirdle asked.

Miss Eells smiled politely. "We're just doing a little wintertime tour of Wisconsin. By the way, do you know anything about these delightful wall paintings?"

Mrs. Bracegirdle sniffed. "I'm glad *you* think they're delightful," she said dryly. "Some of us have a slightly different opinion of them. Now, you take that picture there—the one that shows the weird room with the red idol in it. A little boy was in here the other day with his mother, and he looked at the picture and went into hysterics. Bawled and screamed like anything, and his mom had to take him out." She paused and shook her head grimly. "If you want my opinion, that picture is the work of the devil. And I'm not the only one around here who thinks that way. The mayor and the city council have finally decided to have the whole wall painted over. I've had more than one bad dream that was caused by looking at those cursed pictures late at night, after I'd been working here alone in the building."

Miss Eells turned pale, but she tried to act calm. "Oh, really?" she said with a forced smile. "You never can tell what effect pictures are going to have on people, can you? By the way, this Willis Nightwood—the one who did these paintings—was he a local artist?"

Mrs. Bracegirdle made an awful face, as if she had

just tasted something bitter. "He was a local *lunatic*!" she said angrily. "I remember him quite well, and if anyone ever deserved to be murdered, he did. Of course, nobody ever dared to say anything like that while he was alive. They all bowed and scraped to him because he was filthy rich, and everybody hoped that he would leave a ton of money to the town. However, in the end, all we ever got out of him was this collection of wall paintings, and the clock in the tower of this building that we're standing in now."

"Clock?" said Miss Eells, and her eyes grew bright. She was hoping that she would find out something that would be helpful in solving the mystery.

Mrs. Bracegirdle jerked her thumb toward the ceiling. "Yes indeed! Old Willis gave us our town hall clock. I don't know how much it cost, but it's quite a production. The works came from Germany, and the face shows the phases of the moon and all sorts of useless folderol. There used to be two figures up there, too, big ugly things that were supposed to represent a couple of giants from the Bible—Gog and Magog, I think their names were. Anyway, the giants had clubs and they used them to strike the hours on bells. But the machinery that ran the giants broke down, so they were taken out of the clock tower and stored in the basement. But do you know what? About a week ago, somebody broke in and swiped them!"

Again, Miss Eells felt nervous and frightened. Something strange was going on here, that was for certain. Clock figures . . . how on earth did *they* fit into this insane, mixed-up puzzle? *Clock figures.* Something was stirring in the back of Miss Eells's mind. It was like almost being able to remember somebody's phone number, or the name of someone you used to know. *Clock figures* . . . what was it? Oh, well. If there had been some sort of clue floating around in her brain, it was gone now.

"Are you all right?" asked Mrs. Bracegirdle.

Suddenly Miss Eells realized that she had been staring vacantly into space. She blushed and looked sheepish. "I . . . I was just wondering whether I turned off all the burners of my gas stove when I left home today. I'm rather careless about things like that. Well, thank you for all the information," she said briskly. "Anthony and I are going to poke around up here for a couple of days and then head back to Hoosac. It was very pleasant talking to you."

Mrs. Bracegirdle smiled and watched the two of them go, but secretly she was wondering what on earth they were up to. Stillwater certainly wasn't a tourist attraction in the winter, or at any time of the year. Oh well, she thought, they don't look like bank robbers. And with that she turned and went back to her office to work.

With thoughtful frowns on their faces Miss Eells and Anthony trotted down the front steps of the town hall, and then they both turned and looked up at the clock tower. As Mrs. Bracegirdle had said, the face of the clock was full of little cutout spaces where moons and suns went in and out. And below the face were the two empty niches where the figures had stood, and the two tongueless bells that had once tolled the hours.

Miss Eells wrinkled up her nose, and she shook her head violently. "Well!" she said emphatically as she turned away. "There is definitely *something* going on around here, but what? And what on earth did those clock figures make me think of?"

"You got me!" said Anthony, shrugging. He glanced doubtfully over his shoulder. "Do . . . you think that Mrs. Whosis in there knows more than she's letting on?"

Miss Eells smiled sadly and shook her head. "I don't think she knows much more than we do. And right now she is probably wondering what the two of us are doing up in this godforsaken wilderness in the dead of winter. But look—we're not getting anywhere. There's a sandwich shop across the street, and I think we should go there and grab a quick lunch. After that we can do a little more exploring and then head back home. We have gathered some fascinating information, but I'm afraid Emerson will have to interpret it. Right now I feel my tummy rumbling. Come on—let's go feed our faces."

Miss Eells and Anthony went across the street to a coffee shop and had some hot chicken soup and a couple of tomato-and-cheese omelets with toast and jelly. After that they climbed into the Dodge and drove out to Stillwater Lake, which was about three miles outside town. They parked in a lot used by men who went ice fishing on the lake, and then they walked a little way out onto the snow-covered ice. In the distance they could see a small island covered with bare trees. Above the trees rose a tall gray tower that had battlements on top, like a castle. The tower had a few narrow pointed windows, but they were boarded up.

"Well, there it is!" said Miss Eells sourly. "Willis Nightwood's charming summer cottage. Can you imagine going out there to have fun?"

Anthony shook his head. Then he threw a doubtful glance at Miss Eells. "Are we gonna go out there?" he asked in a faltering voice.

"No!" said Miss Eells loudly and firmly. "Some other day perhaps, but not today. The sun is going down, and it gets dark fast up here at this time of year. I want to take a quick drive past Nightwood's old home, and then we're going to skedaddle back to warm safe Hoosac. Brrrhh! The wind out here is getting fierce! Let's go!"

In silence the two of them walked back to the parking lot. The cold red sun had sunk behind the trees on the far side of the lake, and the shadows under the pine trees deepened and spread. Anthony felt glad to be back in the padded warmth of the car, and he sighed with relief when the engine started. He would not have enjoyed being stuck out here in this dark, deserted place. They drove back to Stillwater, and stopped at a Texaco station to fill up the gas tank and get directions. According to the station attendant, the old Nightwood place was out on Three Rod Road. You turned right after the fire station, and if you drove for a mile and a half, you couldn't miss it.

"It's a brick farmhouse with a brick barn next to it," said the man as he took the money that Miss Eells handed to him. "You don't see many brick barns in this part of the country. And in the field out behind the house there's this hill, only it's really not a hill, it's—"

"Thanks, but I know all about the tomb with the scarecrow," said Miss Eells, cutting him off. "That is, I know all that I want to know about it." Quickly she rolled up the car window, but as she was turning the key in the ignition, a thought occurred to her. "Oh, by the way!" she called, as she rolled the window back down. "Do the Swiggerts still live out there?"

The attendant gave Miss Eells a peculiar look. "No," he said, shaking his head. "They just took off one day, and now the place is owned by a lady named Warmish. Mrs. G. Warmish she calls herself, and nobody knows what the G stands for—probably Griselda, or somethin' really awful like that. She's an odd duck, and she keeps pretty much to herself. I see her in here about once a week, when she does her shoppin'. Why'd you ask?"

Miss Eells felt a cold pool of fear in her heart. For some reason, this news disturbed her. "Oh . . . uh, no reason, no reason at all," she said, smiling weakly. "I'm just nosy by nature. Thanks for your information, and I hope the new year is good to you."

"Same to you!" said the man, smiling, and he waved cheerfully as they drove off.

Miss Eells's old Dodge rolled down the snowy street. Following the gas station attendant's directions, she turned right after the firehouse, and Anthony saw a signpost that said THREE ROD ROAD. The streetlights were behind them now, and the beams of the car's headlights reached out into the night. Anthony felt tense, and he knew that Miss Eells did too—she had not said a word since they left the gas station.

"Miss Eells?" said Anthony, speaking up suddenly. "Why don't we just go on back to Hoosac? We don't really have to look at that old farmhouse, do we?"

After a long pause Miss Eells answered. "I just think we ought to have a look," she said quietly. "We may be on the trail of something, and it just seems that old Nightwood's farm is the logical place to look next. I'd like to ask this Mrs. Warmish a couple of questions."

They drove past tall snowy banks and bare skeletal trees. Finally, after they had rounded a curve, they saw it: a two-story brick house with a stone porch. The downstairs windows glowed yellow, and a gray, ghostly curl of smoke rose from the tall chimney. Behind the house, lost in the darkness, lay the tomb where the lamp once had been buried.

"There it is," said Anthony as their car slowly approached the house. His voice was throaty and weak and a bit trembly.

"Yes," Miss Eells began, "and maybe—" Suddenly she stopped talking and swerved the car onto the shoulder of the road. She switched off the lights and sat breathing heavily in the darkness. At first Anthony was too startled to say anything, but now he saw why Miss Eells had stopped. A car was backing out of the driveway next to the house. As Anthony and Miss Eells watched breathlessly, the car bumped and jounced onto the road. It was moving forward, heading straight toward them. Its headlights were like two cold, frosty moons, and they saw the shadow of the driver's head. Then the car swept past them and was gone.

Miss Eells heaved a deep sigh of relief. "Good heavens!" she exclaimed. "I'm *so* glad she didn't see us!"

Anthony very much wanted to get away, but he was afraid Miss Eells had something else in mind. "Whadda we do now?" he asked nervously.

Miss Eells did not answer. She started the car and drove forward toward the well-shoveled driveway.

"Are you gonna go *in* there?" Anthony asked in a voice that was almost a yelp.

"I am indeed," said Miss Eells firmly. "I have got

some funny ideas in my head about this Mrs. G. Warmish, and I'd like to see if I'm crazy or not. Let's hope that she'll stay away for a while."

Anthony wanted to jump out of the car and run off down the frozen road. But he stayed put as Miss Eells eased the Dodge up the rutty driveway and parked next to the front porch of the house. She turned off the motor and the lights, and they both got out and padded up the front steps. Boldly Miss Eells stepped forward and seized the cold china knob of the front door. She twisted it and the door opened.

The hallway was warm and smelled of wood smoke. Two lovely hooked rugs lay on the floor, and against the wall stood an elaborate old mahogany coat tree. A door on the left stood ajar, and a bright bar of light fell across the hall floor. Miss Eells and Anthony went in through the doorway, and they found that they were in a beautifully furnished parlor. Antique chests and dressers stood against the walls, and a grandfather clock ticked quietly in the corner. In the middle of the room was a polished oak table, and on it burned a nickel-plated electric lamp with a scalloped green glass shade. Propped open on the table was a small battered book, and next to it was a sheet of paper on which a single sentence had been written. Curious, Miss Eells moved closer to the table and bent over to inspect the writing. It was in a foreign language, but Miss Eells knew what it said because she had taken a course in Anglo-Saxon in graduate school years ago. Slowly she moved her finger over the strange letters:

Hwenne tha mōna in Māerċ ġefyllede is, thonne cometh Aesctaroth, ond micel wundor gewyrcath.

Anthony had moved to Miss Eells's side. "What does it say?" he asked.

Miss Eells shook her head in a puzzled way. "As far as I can figure out," she said, "it means this: *When the moon is full in March, then Ashtaroth will come, and will work a great wonder*. Ashtaroth is the ancient Phoenician goddess of the moon, but I don't think I ever heard that the Anglo-Saxons worshipped her. This is very, very peculiar and mystifying." She glanced quickly at the book, and saw that all of it was written in the Anglo-Saxon language. The passage that had been copied out was underlined in red.

"Ashtaroth!" Miss Eells repeated as she glanced around at the fancy antique furniture. "*Ashtaroth!* What on *earth* is going on? What can all this possibly mean?"

Anthony was getting more nervous by the minute. Anxiously he tugged at the sleeve of Miss Eells's coat. "Come on!" he said. "We hafta get outta here before that old lady—"

"Oh, Anthony, *shush*!" said Miss Eells irritably. "Stop being so antsy and let me prowl and snoop a bit. I want to find out if there's any connection between this Warmish woman and Mrs. Grimshaw. If I can find a desk with some letters on it, then maybe we can clear up part of this mystery and have a few more tidbits to offer Emerson when we see him again. So entertain yourself—we're not leaving yet!"

Anthony threw a despairing glance at his friend, and then he turned and walked down a short hall to the kitchen. In it he found an old-fashioned iron cookstove, a shelf full of groceries, and a table with a white enameled top. Next to the stove was a door with a calendar hanging on it, and when he opened it, Anthony saw rickety wooden stairs leading down. After pausing briefly to switch on the cellar light, he began to pick his way from one creaky step to another. A strong smell of earth rose to his nostrils, and when he got to the bottom of the steps, Anthony found that he was in an old-fashioned cellar with a dirt floor. Wooden crates full of vegetables lay here and there, but in the middle of the floor a large hole had been dug. And sticking out of the hole were the head and shoulders of a large red statue. It was the statue of a woman with bulging red-veined eyes; gilded Greek letters were stamped on her forehead. Entwined in the golden hair of the statue was a silver crescent moon, and her left hand pointed at her forehead. The woman's other arm was still buried in the earth up to the shoulder, but Anthony could see the tip of a golden sceptre.

For about half a minute Anthony stood and stared. Then he raced back up the stairs, through the kitchen, and into the living room, where he found Miss Eells going through the drawers of an old walnut sideboard.

"Miss Eells!" Anthony exclaimed breathlessly. "For gosh sakes, come on! I wanta show you something! It's a statue like . . . like the one in the painting. Come see!"

Miss Eells was startled, but she closed the drawer and followed Anthony back through the kitchen and down the cellar stairs. At the bottom she paused and gasped.

"Holy mother of God!" she exclaimed. "Now *that* is not the sort of thing you find in the basements of farmhouses every day! Wait till Em hears about this! And then let him try to claim that there isn't anything odd going on up here! Sweet Georgia Brown, isn't that something!" Miss Eells let out a low whistle and she shook her head slowly. Finally she turned and led Anthony back up the steps. She switched off the cellar light, and then the two of them made their way back through the house to the front door.

"I am *very* glad we're leaving!" said Miss Eells as she stepped out onto the front porch. "This place was beginning to give me the creeps, even before I saw the statue. Come on!"

Quickly Miss Eells and Anthony began to move along the shoveled walk toward the driveway. Anthony happened to glance to the left, and he stopped short. Grabbing Miss Eells's arm, he made her halt too.

"Good grief, Anthony, what is it *now*?" she snapped. "This is not a time to be pointing out—"

Miss Eells stopped speaking. She had seen what Anthony was looking at. Not far away, in the middle of the snow-covered yard, was an old-fashioned well with a high stone curb and a little roof mounted over it on posts. It looked like a fairy-tale wishing well, and it even had a winch and a brassbound wooden bucket hanging from a rope. Shining up out of the well was a mottled, greenish, watery light. Although the light was faint, it illuminated the well and made it stand out in the darkness.

"Well now, that is strange!" said Miss Eells in a wondering and fearful voice. "Do you suppose there's some kind of heating gadget down inside the well, to keep the water from freezing? Otherwise, I can't imagine why . . ."

Again Miss Eells's voice died, and she began to walk off through the deep snow toward the well. Anthony followed her. He really had no choice in the matter, because they both had been seized by a powerful desire to see the source of the light that was shining up out of the well. It was more than a desire—it was as if some irresistible force was dragging them forward. It was awkward for the two of them to stump along through the deep snow, but finally they reached the well and peered in. The surface of the water was ripply, but below were clear lighted depths. At the bottom of the well they saw skeletons and drowned bodies, and among the pale bloated corpses, they saw themselves, Anthony and Miss Eells, lying side by side in death. Suddenly they felt themselves being grasped by powerful unseen hands. They tried to cry out, but they had no voices, and in spite of their frantic struggles they were dragged over the rough stone edge of the well curb and were thrust into the depths of the icy water. Instantly they both blacked out.

CHAPTER NINE

When Miss Eells came to, she was sitting in the old mud-spattered Dodge, which was hurtling down a dark country road at great speed. To her astonishment her foot was on the accelerator and her hands gripped the wheel tightly. She glanced quickly to her right and saw that Anthony was sitting beside her. He was shaking his head and glancing blearily around, like someone who had just awakened from a long sleep.

"Wha . . . wha . . ." mumbled Anthony thickly. "Wha's goin' on?"

"Oh Lord above! I wish I knew!" exclaimed Miss Eells as she took her foot off the accelerator and began pumping the brake. The car began to slow down, and she finally brought it to a skidding stop at the side of the road. For the first time Miss Eells noticed that the car's headlights were off, and with a frightened gasp she reached out and switched them on.

"Oh my heavens!" muttered Miss Eells as she made the sign of the cross. "What if we had hit somebody while we were zooming along without lights like that? What happened to that well, and the corpses? Weren't we drowning a few seconds ago? This is awful! Just awful!" As Anthony watched, Miss Eells opened the car door and got out. She began to pace back and forth on the road, and as she paced she rubbed her face and shook her head. Finally she came back to the car, got in, and slammed the door. Her fingers gripped the ignition key, and the motor roared to life.

"Where are we?" asked Anthony. He still felt totally dazed and frightened.

"Well you may ask," said Miss Eells bitterly as the car began to move forward again. "For all I know we may be in Nebraska or Canada. On the other hand, this road seems vaguely familiar, so I'll take a wild guess and say that we're probably on good old Three Rod Road, heading back toward Stillwater. Also, I see that the gas tank is nearly full, so we couldn't have done too much gallivanting around in the night. I'm going straight back to Stillwater so we can find the road that goes south, and then we're going to drive till we reach Hoosac. How are you feeling?"

Anthony rubbed his legs with his hands. "I feel kind of fuzzy in the head and numb all over, but I guess I'm okay," he said uncertainly. "What happened? Why did it look like we were gonna drown, and are we awake now or havin' a dream or what?"

"I think we are more or less awake and in our right minds now," said Miss Eells grimly. "And as you may have noticed, our clothes are not even damp. That scene at the well was an illusion, something that was meant to scare us half to death. Mrs. G. Warmish—or whatever her name is—was trying to make us so scared that we'd never go back and pry into her affairs again. Of course, if we had gotten killed while we were hurtling along this dark road in a car without lights, I don't suppose Mrs. Warmish would have minded much. So why didn't she kill us outright?" Miss Eells sighed deeply and shrugged. "Ah well," she went on, "that is one of the questions that we will have to toss into Emerson's lap when we see him again. In the meantime, if you know any nice long-distance driving songs, I wish you would sing them."

Around midnight, Miss Eells's Dodge came chugging into Hoosac. The two travelers were dead tired, but their nerves were still atingle from the frightening thing that had happened to them out at Mr. Nightwood's old home. When they got to his house, Anthony climbed out, mumbled "Thank you" to Miss Eells, and stumbled on up the walk to his front door. He climbed the stairs, pulled off his shoes, and threw himself into the bed without even pulling the spread back. He slept soundly, but he had a disturbing dream about wandering around an enormous cemetery late at night. Somehow he found his way down a long stone ramp to a strange underground bathroom with hundreds of rooms in it. Anthony walked and walked, past gloomy ill-lit chambers where cracked marble tubs gaped and greenish copper faucets dripped endlessly. As he went, he began to hear footsteps behind him, and he ran faster and faster till he came to a flight of stone stairs that led down to two grim nail-studded doors. As Anthony watched in numb horror, the doors opened to reveal an empty satin-lined coffin in a room where rows of grandfather clocks stood along the walls. But instead of ordinary clock faces, these gloomy giants had grinning moon faces like the one Anthony had seen in the farmhouse. The footsteps got closer and closer, and unseen hands seized Anthony and thrust him into the coffin. The lid clicked shut over his face, and as he screamed and pounded, the coffin was lowered down, down, down . . . and then, blessedly, he awoke.

The New Year came in with icy winds and snowstorms. Anthony followed his usual daily routine of school, homework, and household chores. In the evenings, when he was shelving and sorting books at the library, he often had conversations with Miss Eells, but they weren't very satisfying. For some reason she did not want to talk about their trip to Stillwater, the haunted oil lamp, or the webby-faced ghost. She did say that she had called Emerson to tell him about the strange things that had happened to them up in Stillwater, and the weird painting they had seen in the town hall, but she would not say what Emerson thought. As time passed, Anthony began to get worried, and before long he was positively alarmed. It was not like Miss Eells to clam up like this. He shared his secrets with her, and she was always open and honest with him. What was she scared of? Or was she under a spell of some sort? Anthony desperately wanted to know what she thought about the Nightwood case, but it was like trying to open a sardine can without the key. She just wouldn't talk.

One freezing cold day toward the end of February, Anthony was cleaning the windows in the East Reading Room. It was Saturday, the only day when he worked mornings, and he was busily squirting Windex on grimy panes and swabbing them with an old rag. Outside, cars rolled past on the icy streets, and little flakes of snow twirled down from the leaden clouds overhead. Suddenly Anthony stopped what he was doing and stared. A black 1938 La Salle had pulled up to the curb outside the library. As far as Anthony knew, only one person in the world drove a car like that: Emerson Eells. As Anthony watched, the little man jumped out of his car, shut the door, and came trotting jauntily up the walk. He wore a camel's hair coat with a fur collar and a green Alpine hat, and under his arm he carried a large leather portfolio that was fastened by a wide leather strap. Anthony put down the Windex bottle and the rag, and he ran to the main foyer of the library, where the big paneled circulation desk stood. A set of wood-framed swinging doors opened into the room, and they swung open with a quack-quack sound. In walked Emerson. He was red-faced and out of breath, and he looked very upset. Emerson was normally the calm, cool, and collected type, and so naturally Anthony wondered what on earth was up.

"Hello, Anthony, how . . . how are you?" gasped Emerson as he glanced distractedly around. "Where is my sister? Eh?"

Anthony discovered that Emerson's nittiness was catching—he began to stammer and act flustered himself. "She's . . . she's in her office, sir," he said, jabbing his finger toward the back of the building.

Emerson pulled himself together and grinned wryly. "Anthony," he said solemnly, "I am not 'sir' to you, but your old friend Emerson, so I wish you'd address me as such. I didn't mean to alarm you by bursting in here this way, but I have something important to discuss with Myra, and with you. Can you tear yourself away from your work and come back to her office with me?"

Anthony glanced around quickly. Old Mr. Beemis was

in the East Room reading *National Geographic*. In the West Reading Room two twelve-year-old boys were quietly playing a game of chess. He wouldn't be needed for the next ten minutes or so. With Emerson close behind him, Anthony walked down a long narrow corridor and banged with his fist on a paneled oak door.

"Come in!" called Miss Eells.

Anthony opened the door and stepped aside to let Emerson in. Miss Eells was sitting at her desk, which was littered with white cards. A long wooden drawer lay near her elbow, and across it a long brass rod was propped. Miss Eells was trying to reorganize the card catalog of the library. She had been at this job for several years, but she had only made it as far as the letter C because she hated to work on the catalog and was always finding other things to do instead. When she looked up and saw Emerson her jaw dropped, and then she grinned happily.

"Em!" she exclaimed, jumping up. "This is wonderful! Why didn't you call and tell me you were coming? I would have . . ." Miss Eells's voice trailed away. She could see from the look on her brother's face that something was wrong. Very wrong. "What's up?" she asked in a weak, throaty voice.

"Well you may ask," muttered Emerson as he dumped the heavy portfolio on the desk. "Anthony, come on in and shut the door."

Emerson took off his coat and hat and hung them in

the closet. Then he walked back to the desk and sat down in the leather-upholstered chair. Leaning forward, he undid the buckle on the strap that held the portfolio shut. He reached in and pulled out a set of watercolor drawings that were mounted on heavy cardboard mats. Anthony crowded in close for a look, and Miss Eells leaned forward in her chair.

Emerson cleared his throat. "These," he said as he tapped the pile of drawings with his finger, "are pictures of the insides of various rooms in Willis Nightwood's summer home on the island out in the middle of Lake Stillwater. It seems that the house was not always the gloomy boarded-up dump that is there now. Nightwood actually threw parties, if you can believe it, and he invited poets, painters, musicians, and other cultural hotshots to his place. I found this out from an elderly librarian in the Archives Department of the University of Minnesota library. I was up there doing some legal research, and I happened to mention Willis Nightwood to him, and then I really got an earful. Later he took me right to the drawings, which probably haven't been looked at in years." Emerson reached into the middle of the pile and slid out a drawing that showed an elaborately furnished room full of overstuffed couches and chairs with tall gilded backs and scrolled arms. In the middle of the room was a large circular couch with a high tufted back. It was the kind of couch that is sometimes seen in art museums. There were no windows in the room, but a marble fireplace was set in one wall, and above it were two niches that held urns. Another niche was set high up on the left-hand wall, and it seemed to hold something, though it was hard to see what it was.

Emerson folded his hands in his lap and stared at the drawing for a long time. Then he glanced quickly up at Miss Eells. "Does this room remind you of anything?" he asked.

Miss Eells looked blank. "No," she said. "Should it?"

Emerson glowered at his sister, and then he threw himself back in his chair and waved his arm scornfully. "Merciful sweet heavens!" he exclaimed. "Can't anybody ever see *anything*? This room is a lot like the room in the weird painting that you saw in the Stillwater town hall! The painting you told me about—remember? Those niches over the fireplace could hold statues and not urns. The niche in the wall to the left could very well be a window, and that couch in the middle of the room could hide a round pedestal, the kind the lamp was sitting on. Is it clear to you now?"

Miss Eells frowned and shook her head slowly. "I don't know, Em. I really don't know. There are a lot of *could be*'s and *might be*'s in what you're saying. What about the red statue? The one we saw in Mrs. Warmish's basement? Would there be room for it on the mantel of that fireplace?"

"There would be room if somebody decided to *make*

room for it," said Emerson through clenched teeth. He was getting more annoyed by the minute. "Mother of heaven, Myra!" he exclaimed, jabbing his finger at Miss Eells. "*This* is the room! The one in the painting! I'd bet any amount of money on it!"

Anthony stared at Emerson in amazement. He had never seen him this worked up before. Miss Eells was rubbing her lower lip doubtfully.

"You always did get crabby when you couldn't have your own way," she said, grinning at her brother. Then her manner changed. She folded her hands on her desk, leaned forward, and looked serious. "But," she added, "you're a very clever man and you may be on to something. All right then. Let's say that you're right. The room in the picture here could be fixed up to look like the room in the weird wall painting. So what?"

"Yeah," added Anthony as he leaned forward to tap the picture with his finger. "Does that mean old Mr. Whosis did evil witchcraft ceremonies at his summer place? Is that what the statues and the magic lamp and the altar are for?"

Emerson's face lit up. He was absolutely delighted. "Anthony!" he crowed, jumping up and slapping him on the back. "Very good! Very *good*! You're a brilliant young man with a quick and discerning mind. The room was for ceremonies that old Willis was *going* to perform someday. But apparently he was missing one or two of the ingredients for his ghastly occult recipe. He had the lamp, he had the red statue, he had the two figures that had been installed as clock jacks in the town hall—"

"*Jacks!*" exclaimed Miss Eells, interrupting. "*That's* what the clue on the tomb door means! Animated figures that strike the hours are called clock jacks! I almost thought of that up there in Stillwater, but I just couldn't come up with the word!"

"You should take lessons to improve your vocabulary," said Emerson dryly. "If you're through interrupting, I'll go on. Old Nightwood needed something—I don't know what—in order to do his hocus-pocus. While he was trying to find the missing thing, he let the jacks stay in the clock tower, and he buried the red statue in his basement. Later he may have tried to get the things he wanted by using *another* magic ceremony, and maybe that is why an evil spirit took possession of his body. At any rate there is somebody up there in Stillwater now who is getting ready to do the magic right, and we can't let that happen. You see—"

"I don't mean to seem dense, Em," said Miss Eells, cutting in again, "but *what* is this lunatic planning to do?"

Emerson gave his sister an exasperated look. "If you'll let me, I'll tell you. Remember that sentence in Anglo-Saxon that you found scrawled on a piece of paper in Nightwood's house? Well, it's from an ancient book of magic called *Aelfrics Wuldor*. A few manuscripts of this book existed in England in the ninth century, and I have a copy. Somehow Saxon wizards found out about Ashtaroth, the Phoenician goddess of the moon. They believed that Ashtaroth's spirit had been cast into the outer darkness thousands of years ago. But it was always waiting to return, and it *could* return if the proper ceremonies were acted out at the right time. The trouble was the Saxons didn't know how to bring her back. But they had seen visions and read signs in the heavens, so they knew what would happen if she did come back to earth and take human form."

"What?" asked Anthony breathlessly.

Emerson gave Anthony a quick, frightened glance. He jumped up and began to pace back and forth on the carpet. Then he stopped and stared piercingly at Anthony. "My young friend," he began, slowly, "how would you like it if there was someone walking around among us who could kill you with a glance—I mean, *really* kill you, stone cold dead? And what if that same person could go anywhere just by thinking? What if that person could know the thoughts of everyone for miles around and invade your mind and fill it with horrid unnameable thoughts and hideous blood-freezing fears? What if that person could become invisible and commit crimes and never get caught?"

Anthony turned pale. "There couldn't be a person like that, could there?" he asked in a trembling voice.

Emerson bit his lip. "Most people nowadays would say that a creature like that could not possibly exist. But most people might be wrong. Ashtaroth is just an ancient name for an evil spirit from the outer darkness, a spirit of unimaginable power and cruelty. That woman in the farmhouse up in Stillwater is trying to bring Ashtaroth back—actually, she is trying to *become* Ashtaroth. When she made you think you were drowning in a well full of skeletons, she was using some of Ashtaroth's powers. But what if Mrs. Warmish could play nasty tricks like that whenever she felt like it? She could make life a nightmare for anybody that she didn't like." Emerson paused and stared hard at a calendar on the wall. "I don't know what is going to happen in Stillwater when the moon is full in March," he said quietly, "but I will be there, and I will try to stop it if I possibly can."

CHAPTER TEN

There was silence in Miss Eells's office for a long time. The small ormolu clock on the shelf by the window ticked loudly, and from outside came the muffled sound of cars passing the building. Emerson went back to his chair and sat down. He took a small plastic comb from his pocket and began running his thumb over the teeth—a nervous habit he had acquired long ago.

"For the love of heaven, stop *doing* that!" exclaimed Miss Eells irritably. "Why don't you crack your knuckles, like a normal person?"

"Never learned how," muttered Emerson, smiling faintly. "Besides, whoever said I was normal?"

"Nobody!" snapped Miss Eells. She heaved a deep

despairing sigh, shoved her chair back, and gripped the arms tightly. "Em," she said, slowly and gravely, "I believe that what you've told us is true. But what in the name of heaven can we do? That woman handled Anthony and me pretty well. She could probably have killed us outright. What makes you think we can stop her from becoming a superhuman demonic being, if that's what she wants?"

Emerson slid his comb back into his pocket and rubbed his hands over his face. "You have a point," he said at last. "We may not be able to stop her, but we are bloody well going to have a try at it! The moon is full on the tenth of March, which is in about two weeks. If we go up to Stillwater then, we may be able to interrupt the ritual while it's in progress. By the way, who is this Mrs. G. Warmish, anyway?"

"I was wonderin' about that too," put in Anthony, who was feeling a bit left out of the conversation.

Miss Eells glowered at them both. "Well, don't come to *me* for answers, you two! Who do you think I am, Dr. IQ? Mrs. Warmish must be the one who swiped the lamp from Adele Grimshaw after Adele stole it from the closet in the chemistry lab. And then she probably used the evil magic of the lamp to kill Adele. Maybe Mrs. Warmish was the one who tunneled into the tomb and took the lamp in the first place. Then she sold the lamp to Adele, and later, somehow, she found out that the lamp had incredible powers. When she went to get it back, she turned poor Adele into powder. Does that sound like a reasonable explanation?"

Emerson stared thoughtfully at the carpet. "It's reasonable," he muttered, "but that doesn't mean it's right. Adele must have thought the lamp was evil and that's why she sold it to you. But we still don't know why she wanted the lamp back. And what about the money that Adele took out of the bank before she was killed? There are a lot of puzzling questions that are, as yet, unanswered. But the important point is, this Warmish woman has got to be stopped, and I'm the one who's going to do it!"

Miss Eells glanced skeptically at her brother. "A minute ago you said that *we* were going to go up to Stillwater and stop Mrs. Warmish. Now you're saying 'I'm going to do it.' So which is it, Em? Us or just you?"

Emerson looked flustered. Then he drew himself up and folded his arms stubbornly. "If you must know, Myra," he said finally, "I think that I ought to go up there by myself. This is going to be pretty dangerous business, and . . . well, the two of you would just get in the way and make things even more perilous."

If looks could kill, Anthony and Miss Eells would have wiped out Emerson on the spot. No one said anything for a full minute, but then finally Miss Eells spoke. "Get in the way, would we?" she sniffed indignantly. "I can see why you'd want Anthony to stay behind, but I'll be darned if I'll sit at home crocheting doilies while you risk your neck up there alone! I'm an old woman and I know I stick my foot into wastebaskets sometimes, but I'm your only sister and I've been your helper through thick and thin all of our lives, and you're not going to leave me out of this! *Do you hear?*"

At the end of this little speech, there were hot angry tears in Miss Eells's eyes, and her voice was trembling. Emerson's face got red, and he stared hard at the floral pattern on the rug. "Well, Myra," he muttered, "I . . . I suppose I could take you along. But I really couldn't answer for your safety."

Now it was Anthony's turn to be angry. "You mean you're gonna leave me behind because I'm a dumb teenager who doesn't know how to blow his nose?"

Emerson stiffened. "I never said you were stupid, Anthony. But I would not be able to forgive myself if something happened to you. We're not going on a jolly jaunt in the country, you know. We're going to wrestle with the powers of darkness. If you knew what you were getting into, you would be very glad to stay at home here in Hoosac. Believe me, you would!"

Anthony didn't agree with Emerson, and he tried to argue, but in the end he got nowhere. Emerson said that Anthony could come to Miss Eells's house and see them off, but that was the most he was willing to let Anthony do. And he added that he would need help from both of them if his plan was going to succeed.

"I'll help you if I can!" said Miss Eells with a despairing sigh. "But I'd still like to know what on earth you think you can do. I want some sort of reasonable plan from you."

Emerson blushed and glanced away quickly. "I don't have a plan yet," he snapped. "But when I do, you two will be the first to know about it. Till then I want you both to promise me that you won't say *anything* to *anybody*." He turned to Anthony and glared at him over the tops of his glasses.

"Sure—I promise," said Anthony in a small, frightened voice.

"How about you, Myra?" asked Emerson, turning to his sister.

"I am not a blabbermouth," said Miss Eells, eyeing her brother coldly. "If there is one in this family, it's you! Why, I remember when—"

"All right! Enough!" exclaimed Emerson, clapping his hands over his ears. "I believe. I'm sure you won't tell a soul!" He sighed and dropped his hands into his lap. "Very well. You both are sworn to secrecy. I'll go up to St. Cloud and bury myself in my law books. I'll see you both again when the moon is nearly full."

Time passed. Anthony circled the tenth of March on the calendar that hung on his bedroom door, and he often stared at the smiling, mocking moon face that was stamped under the number ten. As he walked back and forth between school and home, he thought about the things that Emerson had told them in Miss Eells's office. Anthony hoped that Emerson was wrong. Emerson was a cocky, know-it-all sort of person, and he often pretended that he knew things when he really didn't. So maybe he was wrong this time. Then Anthony thought about what had happened to him and Miss Eells up in Stillwater. If Mrs. Warmish could make them think that they were drowning, then she also had the power to turn Mrs. Grimshaw to dust and to knock him and Miss Eells unconscious without even touching them. A chill passed through Anthony's body. What if that evil, nightmarish creature was listening to his thoughts right now? Anthony gritted his teeth and closed his eyes to get rid of the unpleasant visions that were swarming into his head. *Maybe Emerson is wrong*, he repeated over and over as he walked along. *Maybe Emerson is wrong*. Anthony hoped so. He hoped so with all his heart. But he also hoped that Emerson would change his mind and take him along on the trip up to Stillwater.

Toward the end of the first week of March, Anthony started watching the sky. The nights were clear and cold, and he saw the moon rise every night above the wooded bluffs of the Mississippi. One evening, when he had finished working at the library, he and Miss Eells rode back to his house. Anthony thought that his friend was unusually nervous. She muttered to herself a good deal, and she kept switching stations on the car radio. Finally Anthony couldn't stand it any longer. He had to find out what was going on.

"Are . . . are you tryin' to find some program you like?" he asked hesitantly.

"Yes," she snapped irritably as she twiddled the knob. "I want to find a weather report. Emerson is due here on the evening of the ninth, and today I heard a storm is on its way down from Canada. All we need is three feet of snow blocking the roads when we go to make our move."

Miss Eells searched the dial a bit more, and then she turned off the radio in disgust. "Rot!" she muttered as she swerved around a corner. "They have all sorts of things you *don't* want, like hog and oat prices, but no weather! If I ran a radio station—"

"What's Emerson gonna do?" said Anthony, cutting in. "Has he figured out how to stop that woman?"

Miss Eells grimaced. "I wish you hadn't asked me, though I knew you would, sooner or later. Yes, he called me last night, and—believe it or not—he's going to dynamite the place."

"*Dynamite!*" exclaimed Anthony. He blinked in astonishment. "Does he know how to use—"

"He thinks he does," said Miss Eells, scowling. "We have a cousin who's in the construction business, and Em has watched him blast tree stumps and rocks, and so he thinks he knows what to do. He wants to sneak into that house on the island sometime in the wee hours of the morning, on the tenth. He figures that by that time Mrs. Ghastly will have her statues and the lamp and all the other paraphernalia set up, and he'll be able to blow everything sky-high, so she won't be able to have a second try next year. I know, I know . . . there are a lot of holes in his great plan, but it's the best one he could come up with. And maybe, with a little luck, it'll work. But it's going to be extremely dangerous, and so I think Emerson was absolutely right when he told you that you couldn't come with us. I'm going because I'm old and silly and Em is my dear brother. But I don't want to be the one who gets you killed. Do you understand?"

Anthony wanted to yell that he would come along, regardless of what she said. But he knew that would just make Miss Eells angry, so he bit his tongue and muttered "Uh-huh." He would wait and watch, and figure out how to stow away in Emerson's car.

On the evening of the eighth of March, it started to snow. Steadily the flakes came down, hour after hour, and by dawn a foot had fallen. When he looked out his bedroom window in the morning, Anthony groaned. His street was a rippled white desert, with humps here and there that hid parked cars. In the distance a snow plow was growling, but it would be late afternoon before it got to the Mondays' house. School would be closed,

and the library too. And the road to Stillwater . . .
Anthony glanced up at the gray sky. More snow would
be coming down. *How on earth were Miss Eells and Emerson ever going to get up there?*

Glumly Anthony plodded down the stairs to the
kitchen. His mother was standing at the stove, making
scrambled eggs, and his dad was sitting at the round oak
table, slowly sipping coffee.

"Hi, folks," sighed Anthony as he sank into a chair.
"Guess we're snowed in today, huh?"

"Kind of looks that way," said Mr. Monday, smiling
ruefully. "Won't be nothin' open today, and there's more
snow on the way. The man on the radio said at least a
foot more, maybe two. I get tired just thinkin' about
shovelin' out the alley behind my saloon."

"You'd better get somebody to help you," put in Mrs.
Monday in a worried voice. "Remember you've got a
bad heart, Howard, and you're not supposed to over-
exert yourself."

Mr. Monday gave Anthony a look, as if to say: I wish
I hadn't brought up the subject of snow shoveling. "Well,
Anthony," he said, after clearing his throat, "whatcha
gonna do with yourself today? Build snowmen?"

Anthony laughed. "Nope. I'm gonna dig those snowshoes outta the attic and go for a walk down the street."
I'll come back and help you shovel later." He did not
add that he was going to snowshoe all the way over to
Miss Eells's house, so he could find out what was going

on with Emerson. He would have called her up, but the telephone was in the front hall, and with both his parents at home, there was a good chance that one of them would overhear him.

"Okay, Tony," said his dad with a cheerful smile and a wave of his hand. "Have a good time, and if you run inta any bears, watch out!"

Anthony laughed and started digging into the plate of scrambled eggs that his mother had just set in front of him.

Later that same morning Anthony was clumping down the snow-covered street on his snowshoes. He had used these odd tennis-rackety things before, and he could move at a pretty good rate of speed. As he walked he glanced around. Old men in red hunting hats were shoveling their walks, and kids were building snow forts. A snowball whizzed past his head, and with a laugh he ducked. Anthony paused to catch his breath. How far had he come? There was the Baptist church with its square white stone tower, so . . .

Anthony looked ahead, and then he gaped. Coming toward him over the snow was Miss Eells. She was wearing a pair of long cross-country skis, and she propelled herself with two stout ski poles. She wore a floppy blue and orange stocking cap with a blue pom-pom and an old padded blue parka with a ratty imitation-fur collar. Her cheeks were very red, and her glasses were slightly askew on her face. Anthony didn't want to laugh, but he did—he couldn't help it. Miss Eells looked like Grandma Moses trying out for the U.S. Winter Olympics.

"Go ahead, mock!" called Miss Eells as she shoved herself closer to him. "Make fun, see if I care!" And then she broke down and laughed herself—she knew how she looked, and it really was very idiotic, the whole idea of her on skis!

When she had stopped laughing, Miss Eells told Anthony that she had heard from Emerson on the phone that morning. ". . . and believe it or not," she went on, with a giggle, "he's coming down by *helicopter*!"

Anthony was astounded. "*Huh*? I didn't know he could fly one of those things!"

Miss Eells sighed and shrugged comically. "Well, he can. You see, he learned in the Army Air Corps during the Second World War. And when the war was over, the one thing in the world that Em wanted to own was a copter. So . . . he bought one. Even in those days, Em was rich, and when he found out that the army was planning to store a lot of its helicopters away in mothballs, he offered to buy one. It took a lot of finagling, but he did finally manage to get a whirlybird. I think he has actually had it up in the air a few times since the war. But be that as it may, he *is* planning to bring the silly crate down here, and he'll be landing in a field near the Hoosac airport some time around midnight. He expects us to be there to meet him."

Anthony's heart leaped. "Hey, he's gonna let me go after all! How come he changed his mind?"

Miss Eells looked pained. "Anthony," she said slowly, "I hate to pull the rug out from under you, but Em has *not* changed his mind. He wants you to be there to see us off because . . . well, you're an old and valued friend, and he wants to say good-bye. To be frank, there's a real chance that he and I won't be coming back, and if that should be the case . . . Do you understand what I'm saying?"

Anthony felt a lump forming in his throat, and tears sprang to his eyes. Right then and there he made a decision: He was going along with them. He would keep quiet, and he would watch for a chance to stow away aboard the helicopter.

Miss Eells saw how upset Anthony was, and she reached out to pat his arm. "Please don't listen to all my talk about not coming back," she said, smiling bravely. "I'm a worrier, and I always imagine that the worst possible thing is going to happen. We'll probably be back with a lot of great stories to tell you after this whole crazy business is over with. I think that by midnight the main roads and streets in Hoosac will be cleared, so why don't you catch a taxi and meet me at the corner of Airport and Henderson roads at about ten minutes before twelve. There's a variety store on Airport Road, and after you've seen us off, you can go there to call a cab to take you back home again. Okay?"

Anthony nodded. Then he awkwardly shook hands with Miss Eells and turned to plod on home.

The day dragged on for Anthony. He read part of next week's American history lesson, and he helped his father shovel the driveway. He played several games of chess with his brother, Keith, who had nothing to do because the garage where he usually worked was closed. Every now and then Anthony turned on the radio and checked the latest weather report. There seemed to be some disagreement among the experts: Some said that more snow was coming, and others claimed that it would be a cold clear night, with a full moon rising sometime after midnight. The hours ticked away, and Anthony got fidgetier and fidgetier. Around six his family had dinner, and Anthony volunteered to help with the dishes. While he was drying the silverware, he told his mother very casually that he might take a late-night walk down to the center of town. Mrs. Monday fussed a bit and told him to watch out for skidding cars when he crossed the street, but she didn't really seem terribly worried. If she only knew, thought Anthony.

At ten minutes after eleven he got his parka out of the closet, laced up his army boots, and tucked the snowshoes under his arm. Out the door he went, into the bitingly cold night air. The sidewalks were still covered with snow, but Anthony walked in the street so he could make pretty good time. He loped along, whistling

"Winter Wonderland." Every now and then he glanced up at the sky, which was crowded with stars. Pretty soon he would be up in Stillwater, and with a tightening in his stomach Anthony wondered if he really would make it back, safe and sound.

After ten minutes of steady walking, he made it to Minnesota Avenue, the main street of the town. Next to City Hall was a little white clapboard building that housed the Oldfield Taxi Co. It only had two cabs, and one of them was sitting outside, with the motor running. Through the plate-glass window Anthony could see the dispatcher sitting at his desk, reading a comic book. A cab driver was standing nearby, sipping a cup of hot coffee. Anthony paused. He wanted to turn and run back home. But he took a deep breath and forced himself to open the rattly front door.

"Ex-Excuse me," he stammered, "but . . . I wonder if you c-could take me to . . . to . . ." He paused and swallowed hard. It was tough getting the words out.

The driver, a big beefy man with a red face, turned and caught sight of Anthony. He glanced down at the snowshoes, and he broke up.

"Hey, Dan!" he roared, pointing. "Get a load o'him. I didn't know the dog sled had made it inta town today!"

Both men laughed, and Anthony cringed. But he stood his ground and waited for the guffawing to die down.

"Just kiddin', son," rumbled the big man as he set his coffee cup down on the desk. "Where ya wanta go, eh?"

"I need to go to the corner of Airport and Henderson roads," muttered Anthony. "Can you take me there?"

"Yeah, sure," said the big man carelessly. He waved to the dispatcher and started for the door. On his way out he turned and called over his shoulder. "See ya when the next dog sled gets here!" And with another laugh the man followed Anthony out the door and slammed it behind him.

Anthony got into the cab and propped the snowshoes up on the seat beside him. He sat back and listened to the *chink-chink* of the snow chains on the cab's tires. Finally, when he saw the mailbox at the corner of Henderson Road, Anthony told the driver to stop and let him out. As the cab pulled away, Anthony glanced across the snowy fields toward the airport. The Hoosac Air Field wasn't very much—just a hanger, a small air strip, and a revolving beacon on a small tower. Two Cessnas stood on the unplowed runway, but the place looked absolutely deserted. Quickly Anthony strapped on the snowshoes and plodded across a rippled field. The beacon's long finger of light swept over his head again and again as he made his way over the powdery snow. It seemed to take forever, but he finally made it to a wire fence that separated Mr. Henderson's cornfield from the airport land. After a little searching, Anthony found a place where the fence had been bent down, and he climbed over. A row of pines grew near the fence, and as he passed them, a small shape on skis slid into view.

"Hi, ho, Anthony!" said Miss Eells as she waved a flashlight's beam in his face. "You made it! Congratulations! My insane brother is due to be landing his eggbeater over by that wrecked barn in about fifteen minutes. We're supposed to wave flashlights so he'll know where to come down, but actually he's going to home in on the airport's beacon and use the lights along Henderson Road to get his bearings, so he won't go too far and land on top of some poor man's garage. Isn't this all absolutely *crazy*?"

Silently Anthony agreed that it was. He slogged steadily toward the barn as Miss Eells shuffled and slid and prodded the snow with her ski poles. She was talking a blue streak, and Anthony knew that she was very, very nervous. He was tense, too, and he wondered for the umpteenth time if he really would have a chance to stow away aboard the copter when Emerson's back was turned. He also wondered why in the world he wanted to go. But it was an overpowering urge, an adventure he wanted to be part of.

The barn rose before them, a black mass of shadows with a crooked cupola on top. Miss Eells was wearing a pack strapped to her back, and she reached into it, pulled out another flashlight, and handed it to Anthony. Switching it on, he peered at his watch. It was twenty minutes to midnight. To save the batteries, he snapped the light off, and the two of them settled down to wait.

CHAPTER ELEVEN

Minutes ticked past. A freezing wind whipped at Anthony's legs, and the long arm of the airport beacon kept sweeping past. Every now and then, Anthony and Miss Eells would peer up at the dark sky, but they couldn't see anything.

"Maybe he's lost," said Anthony gloomily. "Are you *sure* he knows how to fly a helicopter?"

Miss Eells heaved a despairing sigh. "Well, he's *supposed* to know how to fly one! For years he's been boring me with stories of the rescue missions he flew when he was in France after the Normandy invasion. Emerson has a lot of hidden talents—but he also pretends he knows more than he actually does. I really don't know what to think, Anthony. Maybe—"

Miss Eells stopped talking and looked up suddenly. From the blackness above them came the drone of a motor and the whap-whap sound of a helicopter's giant propeller. They could make out little yellow lights, and—to their great joy—a searchlight beam flashed. It wobbled about, played over the ruined barn and a clump of trees, and then settled on the two of them. Anthony began to jump up and down and wave excitedly.

"Hey! Hey, Emerson! Down here!" he yelled.

"Easy, Anthony!" said Miss Eells, laying her hand gently on his arm. "He sees us, and if we're lucky, he won't land on top of us. He made it! I was beginning to have my doubts."

As Anthony and Miss Eells watched, the ungainly aircraft slowly settled down. It had a long khaki-colored fuselage, and the battered U.S. Army star was still apparent. Instead of wheels, a set of steel skis gently crunched on the snow as the copter landed. The wind from the whirling propeller blew gusts of snow across the field, but soon the blades slowed to a halt. The cockpit door opened, and Emerson jumped out. He was all done up in an army fatigue uniform, complete with combat boots and a fatigue cap with a scrunched peak. Anthony had to bite his lip to keep from laughing—Emerson in an army outfit was a most unlikely sight.

Miss Eells was not able to stop herself, and she burst into a fit of giggles.

Emerson strode forward across the snow and stopped in front of her. He folded his arms and tried to look stern. "Well?" he said. "What's so incredibly funny?"

"You!" cackled Miss Eells, and she snickered some more. "You look like my college biology teacher going through basic training!"

Emerson harumphed. "Biology teacher indeed! Now Myra, if you've had your little ho-ho for the evening, I would suggest that we get under way. Anthony, would you help Laughing Girl here off with her skis? We can stow them in the back of the copter. We really ought to get going. Time, as they say, is awasting!"

While Emerson paced back and forth, Miss Eells unslung her pack and put it down in the snow, so she'd have something to sit on. Anthony knelt down and began unbuckling the straps that held her feet to the skis, and when the skis were off, Emerson threw them into the open cockpit door. Then he strode quickly back and pumped Anthony's hand. "Thank you very much for all your help, Anthony," he said brusquely. "I wish I could take you along, but if anything happened to you, I'd never forgive myself. I wouldn't be taking Myra along, but she has ways of twisting my arm. Please try to understand."

Anthony forced a smile and nodded. "Sure . . . I

. . . I understand," he muttered. "I hope everything goes okay."

Emerson rolled his eyes upward. "So do I, Anthony. So do I!" He turned to Miss Eells and took her by the arm. "Come on, Myra," he said. "We'd really better be going."

Miss Eells glanced quickly at Anthony. Her eyes were full of tears, and when she spoke, her voice was trembling. "Good . . . good-bye, Anthony!" she said, waving her hand weakly. "I think you're better off staying here. I really do. We ought to be back tomorrow morning sometime. Don't worry about us. Come on, Em. Let's get moving! I cannot *stand* good-byes!"

With a sinking heart, Anthony stood and watched as they crunched across the snow toward the helicopter. He had waited for his chance, but his chance had not come. Dejectedly he bowed his head, but suddenly he jerked it up again. There on the snow lay Miss Eells's pack! In all the confusion they had forgotten it. Anthony's mind raced. If he rushed forward to tell them, they'd know he was still around. His only hope was to hide here in the dark and wait. Crouching down, Anthony scuttled closer to the copter and hid behind a snow-covered bush. The cockpit door was closed. Anxiously Anthony waited. Any minute now the motor would start, and . . .

The door opened. With a muffled curse, Emerson

leaped out and snapped on a small flashlight. Playing the beam back and forth, he walked to the pack. In a flash Anthony was on his feet. Running bent over he hurled himself toward the helicopter and stopped near the open door. Miss Eells saw him, and she almost yelled. But she stopped herself in time.

"Hurry!" she whispered hoarsely. *"Get in!"*

Anthony crawled quickly to the cargo section in the back of the copter. In the darkness he saw the shapes of wooden boxes, probably the explosives. Crouching down flat on the floor, Anthony held his breath and waited. After what seemed like forever, Emerson came back. The cockpit door slammed and Miss Eells's pack landed behind the seats with a light thump.

"There!" said Emerson with an irritated shrug. "I didn't see Anthony around, so I suppose he's gone back home. I do hope he isn't feeling too hurt."

"Oh, I imagine he'll get over it," said Miss Eells in an odd voice. "Let's get this antique Mixmaster into the air."

Emerson started the engine, and the great propeller began to whirl. The noise was deafening, and the copter vibrated alarmingly. Finally, though, the vibration died down and they rose up into the night sky. This is the craziest thing I've ever done in my life, thought Anthony. Emerson was up in front, humming the "Army Air Corps March," and Miss Eells was saying all the prayers she could remember from her Catholic grade school days. Huddled near the boxes, Anthony imagined the endless acres of snowy land that they were passing over. He shifted a bit and then tried to be as still as possible. Under him the steel floor vibrated to the beat of the engine as the copter whirred on through the night.

A long time passed and still they flew. Anthony never knew exactly when he drifted off to sleep, but it finally happened, and once again he had that strange dream about wandering through an endless cemetery and then down into a vast underground maze full of bathtubs and sinks. Anthony awoke with a jolt just as the copter was settling down on the surface of the frozen lake, and before he could stop himself he exclaimed loudly, "Wha . . . where are we?"

Dead silence. The throbbing of the motor had stopped, and so had the endless whirr of the propeller. Anthony silently cursed himself for being so stupid. Finally he heard Emerson clearing his throat.

"I see that we are not alone!" said Emerson in a biting, sarcastic voice. "Myra, were you aware that we had a stowaway?"

"I didn't have the heart to give him away," said Miss Eells apologetically. "He really wanted very much to come."

Emerson heaved a deep, despairing sigh. "Great! Just great!" he growled. "Very well, Myra. Since you were responsible for letting him come on board, I'm going to insist that you two stay here while I go plant the explosives in that dratted house. You can amuse yourselves by thinking up things to say to Anthony's parents when we bring him back. We'll be lucky if they don't charge us with kidnapping!"

While Emerson fumed, Anthony climbed up to the front of the cockpit and peered out through the curved glass windshield. He saw a frozen lake lit faintly by starlight. In the distance masses of trees bristled, and not far away rose the humped shape of an island and the tall battlemented castle that had been Willis Nightwood's summer home long ago. Then Anthony's jaw dropped. He had expected the old house to be dark, but warm yellow lamplight burned in every window. Had they landed in the wrong place?

"Hey!" he said, in a wondering voice. "What the—"

"What indeed?" snapped Emerson. "The joint seems to be jumping, doesn't it? But jumping with *what*?" He glanced at his wristwatch, which glowed faintly green in the dark. "Four after one," muttered Emerson. "According to the almanac I studied before we left, the full moon is due to rise around half-past one. I thought that I would be able to sneak in and plant the dynamite and set it off by remote control, but that may not be possible. Ah well! If worse comes to worst, I have come prepared. I have a spring-powered hand catapult, and I can light the sticks one by one and shoot them into the evil room through a window—after first smashing the panes with a few well-hurled rocks. Let me see . . . the moon rises from the east at this time of year, and according to my dashboard compass, east is *that* way. So the little window will be on that side of the building. Now to get my gear together. Time's awasting!"

As Anthony and Miss Eells sat watching, Emerson filled his sister's pack with the things he needed and strapped it onto his back. He checked the army automatic pistol he carried in a holster at his belt, and then he gave his sister a quick peck on the cheek. He was ready to go.

"Toodle-oo, Myra!" he said jauntily, as he climbed out of the cockpit door. "If I'm not back in a few minutes, you can . . . well, I'm not sure what you can do."

"Run for our lives!" said Miss Eells sourly. "But let's hope it won't come to that. Good luck!"

The cockpit door closed, and Emerson started off across the ice. His small, purposeful shape grew smaller and smaller and was swallowed up in the dark. Tensely, Anthony and Miss Eells waited. Were all those lights a good sign or a bad one? Anthony didn't know. Was Emerson's plan terrific or harebrained? He didn't know the answer to that question either. Minutes dragged past. Outside the copter's window the wind whipped up ghostly eddies of snow and sent them scurrying across the ice. Anthony's thoughts got gloomier and gloomier, until he was suddenly jolted by the sound of Miss Eells singing in a thin, slightly off-key voice with a Southern twang:

> "Mine eyes have seen the glory
>   of the coming of the Lord;
>   He is trampling out the vintage
>   where the grapes of wrath are stor'd . . ."

Anthony laughed—he couldn't help it, he was so startled. "Hey!" he exclaimed. "Why are you singing that?"

Miss Eells said calmly, "I just sing it when I'm nervous. It's better than screaming and tearing your hair, don't you think?"

Anthony nodded and grinned. Suddenly he felt a lot more confident. If little old Miss Eells could sing in a situation like this, he ought to be able to show a little courage. Miss Eells sang some more, and then Anthony recited as much as he could remember of "Thanatopsis," a poem he was memorizing in school. He was about to start "Casey at the Bat" when he looked out and saw a flashlight's pale beam bouncing along through the night. Emerson was coming back . . . or was he? Fear gripped Anthony's heart—what if it was someone else?

They waited, and the light got closer. It was Emerson. His face, lit from below, looked weird, and it also looked puzzled.

Emerson went around to the side of the copter and opened the door. *"Well!"* he exclaimed loudly. "We were certainly wrong about *this* one!"

Miss Eells was astonished. *"Wrong?"*

Emerson nodded emphatically. "Wrong, sis! About as wrong as anybody could possibly be! The house is full of people who are attending a midwinter ball that is being given by the Stillwater Chamber of Commerce. I'm not kidding! There are punchbowls and goodies and a string orchestra and all sorts of silly matrons in flower-print dresses, and husbands looking uncomfortable in white ties and tails. The whole thing is about as occult and mysterious as an ice cream social!"

Miss Eells was utterly flabbergasted. She opened and closed her mouth, but no sound came out. Finally she found her voice. "But . . . but Em!" she sputtered. "It . . . it *can't* be! There's been a snowstorm, remember? How did all those people get out here?"

"They've got snow plows up here in Stillwater, Myra," said Emerson calmly. "It's just the roads between here and Hoosac that are still blocked. Besides, if some big-wigs want to have a party, it's amazing what can get done in a short time."

Miss Eells's eyes narrowed. There was something fishy about all this as far as she was concerned. "Was Mrs. Warmish there?" she asked suspiciously.

Emerson shook his head and laughed. "No, I'm afraid

not! I asked about her, and from what this one fellow told me, she's a hermit, just as you said. She never comes to public—"

"Now see here, Emerson!" exclaimed Miss Eells defiantly. "Are you trying to tell me that Anthony and I dreamed up the whole thing? About what happened to us outside Mrs. Warmish's house, I mean. Do you think we were temporarily insane?"

Emerson smiled blandly and shook his head. "You and Anthony were very tired, and you were also both extremely nervous about breaking into that nasty old hag's home. I think that you both poked around in her house for a while, and then the two of you fell asleep in the front seat of your car, and one of you had a dream about finding the red idol in the basement and getting pitched into the well. Then, when you woke up, the one that had the dream told it to the other one, and you both thought that the dream stuff had *really happened*! When you're half awake you can believe all sorts of crazy things, and at a time like that the power of suggestion can be very strong. Do you see what I'm trying to say?"

Miss Eells folded her arms and glowered at her brother. "Yes, I see what you're saying," she grumbled, "and I think you're being very clever as usual, but I really wonder if you're right. Did I also dream the part about zooming down the road with my headlights off?"

"No," said Emerson calmly. "I think that really happened. You were still half asleep, and you were discombobulated by the dream that you'd had, and so you drove off without switching on your lights." Emerson paused and sighed. He smiled consolingly and patted his sister on the arm. "Don't get me wrong, Myra," he went on, "I'm just as much to blame for this wild-goose chase as you are. I took the evidence you gave me and whipped up a tale about magic rooms and magic statues and Ashtaroth, and it all seemed very reasonable. *And* it may be true that Mrs. Warmish is messing around with witchcraft in her home right now, but she certainly isn't doing anything out here. Now—"

"Wait a minute!" said Miss Eells sharply, and she jabbed a finger at her brother. "Wait just one *minute*! You told me that Mrs. Warmish had learned to do magic illusions. So how do you know that the party in the castle isn't one of her tricks?"

Emerson smiled broadly and confidently. Without a word, he switched on the overhead light inside the cockpit. Then he unbuttoned the front of his army jacket and lifted out something that hung from his neck by a leather thong. It was a round, shiny, metal box, and it looked a lot like a woman's compact. Popping the lid open, Emerson showed what was inside, a small red piece of baked clay. Cut into the clay were a lot of spindly wedge-shaped marks that Anthony recognized immediately from the history books he had been reading in school. The marks were cuneiform writing, the kind the Babylonians had used.

"This is an ancient Babylonian amulet," said Emerson, tapping the piece of clay with his finger. "It was made to ward off evil spells cast by Ishtar, and Ishtar is just another name for Ashtaroth. The writing on the amulet says, 'I am the bane of Ishtar. If her evil presence is near, I will glow like a burning coal.' Well, when I was at the party in the castle just now, I reached inside my jacket and felt the case that the amulet is in, and it was as cold as ice! I brought the amulet with me so that we would be protected from Ashtaroth's evil powers, and I also wanted to use it as an alarm system, to warn us if danger was near. I am absolutely sure there is no danger here, and I am also sure we were totally wrong about the Ashtaroth business. So, I apologize. I think we all ought to go in and have a cup of punch and then climb into the copter and go home. Are you two ready to come with me?"

Anthony and Miss Eells looked at each other. They wanted to feel relieved about the great danger that had turned out to be imaginary, but they both still felt nervous, and they also felt confused. "I . . . I guess I'd just like to stay here and wait for you two to come back," said Anthony hesitantly. "I don't like parties much, and, well, maybe I could guard the helicopter."

Emerson was amused by this suggestion. "Why, of course you can guard this antique flying machine," he said, and as he spoke, he unslung his pack, pulled open the flap, and reached inside. Then he pulled out his stainless steel hand catapult. It had a pistol grip, and a trough in front where you could put the rocks or sticks you wanted to fling. Anthony saw at once how the weapon worked. You pulled the lever on the side back until the spring of the catapult was scrunched up tight, and then when you were ready to shoot, you pulled the trigger in front of the grip, and that cut the spring loose and hurled the rock or stick a long way.

"Not that I think you'll actually be attacked," said Emerson with a chuckle, as he handed the catapult to Anthony. "But I thought you might feel better if you had this to discourage stray dogs. Myra and I are going to trot over to the ogre's castle so we can socialize a bit, but we won't stay long. We'll be back in a jiffy so we can get back to Hoosac at a halfway decent hour. See you."

And with that, Emerson followed Miss Eells out through the cockpit door. Anthony closed the door and sat down in the pilot's seat. He folded his arms and watched as the two shadowy figures moved across the ice toward the brightly lit castle. Minutes ticked past. Anthony hummed a little tune and studied the wintry landscape. Were they there yet? Miss Eells and Emerson had disappeared in the darkness some time ago. By now they were clinking glasses with the guests and having a high old time. *Why was he so worried?* Anthony couldn't help it, but he was. There was a queasy feeling in his stomach that just wouldn't go away. He began to get impatient. When would they be starting back? Would they bring him cookies and cakes to prove that the party was real, and not just—

Anthony jumped as if someone had stuck him with a pin. He sat up straight in his seat, and his eyes opened wide. For some time he had been staring at the long narrow windows that glowed with yellow light. He had been staring in a bored way, but he was not bored any longer. The lights in the windows had suddenly gone out, and the castle was plunged into darkness.

CHAPTER TWELVE

When Miss Eells and Emerson reached the main entrance of the castle, they found that the wide nail-studded door stood slightly ajar, and a narrow streak of light streamed out across the snowy walk. They went in and walked quickly through a drafty entrance hall, and then trotted up a short flight of steps to a set of double doors that opened into a high-ceilinged vaulted room that was full of light, warmth, noise, and the smell of good things to eat. Guests milled around the long tables and filled their plates with food, and a champagne fountain squirted pale bubbly liquid from twenty spouts. Men in tuxedos chatted with women in flower-printed formal dresses, and on a small platform at the far end of the room, a string quartet played. Immediately Miss Eells's fears vanished. This was about as normal and unmagical a scene as anyone could imagine, and she felt embarrassed to think that she had come all the way up here to stop a sinister and frightening ceremony from taking place.

"Well, Em," she said with a relieved smile, "I will confess that I had my doubts when you came back and told us about this party. I expected to see a bunch of ghouls feasting. Let's just grab a cup of punch and then hike on back. I don't want to leave Anthony alone for too long."

Emerson nodded, and they moved to a table that was covered with trays of deviled eggs, cold ham, and various scrumptious looking hors d'oeuvres. At the far end of the table was a cut-glass punch bowl full of an amber bubbly liquid, and near it stood a distinguished looking elderly lady in a formal gown made of some stiff gold-colored cloth. As Emerson and Miss Eells drew near, the lady dipped a silver ladle into the punch bowl and filled a glass cup. She handed it to Miss Eells, and filled another one for Emerson.

"You certainly aren't dressed for our little party," she said, as she gave Emerson his cup. "But I gather that you were out hiking, and you happened to see the lights, so you stopped by. That, at least, is what one of the other guests told me."

"Yes, that's true," said Emerson, and he harumphed self-importantly. He felt out of place in his army fatigue uniform, even though the people he had met at the door on his first visit had told him he was quite welcome to stop in and mingle with the crowd.

"Ah well," said the lady, smiling placidly, "you shouldn't worry about the way you're dressed. We all make mistakes now and then." She paused, and then suddenly her whole manner changed. Her eyes grew hard, and her lips curled into a nasty sneer. "There's another little mistake that you made," she went on ominously. "That amulet of yours worked perfectly well. The inscription says that it will glow like a burning coal when Ishtar is near. Well, when you were here last, it *glowed*, but it did not give off any *heat*. If you had opened the metal case instead of merely feeling it, you would have seen that the piece of clay was glowing. For Ishtar is here, Ashtaroth is here. *And you two are dust under her feet!*"

These last words burst with incredible force from the mouth of the old woman, who now began to waver and shimmer like something seen through water. Emerson and Miss Eells were frozen with horror. The music died with the sound a record player makes when it has run down, and the room was plunged into darkness.

For several minutes Anthony sat dead still in the cockpit of the helicopter. His eyes were open wide, and he was staring at the mass of shadows that had once been the brightly lit castle. What had happened? Were Miss

Eells and Emerson dead? Anthony felt sick inside, and he felt helpless. He fought against his rising panic and tried to tell himself that something normal had happened, like a blown fuse or a power outage. But there had been candles in some of the windows of the castle, and they had gone out when the other lights were extinguished. Something was wrong, very wrong indeed. Anthony wanted to race to the aid of his friends, but what on earth could he do? Outside the moon was rising over the trees, and by its faint light, Anthony could see the things that Emerson had left behind in the cockpit. Nearby lay the pack full of explosives, and the steel catapult was on the passenger seat. Anthony picked up the catapult and hefted it in his hand. It was just a spring-powered version of the slingshot he had used when he was ten years old. But what could he do with it? If he tried shooting dynamite sticks with it, he would kill Emerson and Miss Eells along with whoever—or whatever—was holding them prisoner. Unless they were already dead. . . . But no! He refused to believe that. With the catapult in his hand and a grim look on his face, Anthony opened the cockpit door and clambered down onto the ice.

Outside the air was bitingly cold, and the wind had started to blow again. Anthony buttoned the top button of his leather jacket and pulled his red leather cap down tight on his head. He plodded across the ice and the humped island loomed closer and closer. After a short trek he was making his way up a narrow path that wound through tall pines. The snow had not been shoveled here, but it had been trampled down. Miss Eells and Emerson had probably taken this route. Before long Anthony came out into a clearing, and he looked up. There was the castle, perched on the highest knob of rock on the little island. By the moonlight Anthony could see that most of the castle's windows were still boarded, just as they had been when he and Miss Eells visited here in December. So how could they have been blazing with light a few minutes ago? Anthony felt cold fear in his stomach. He wanted to turn and run away, but with a wrenching shudder he pulled himself together. Gripping the handle of the catapult tightly, he began to climb the snowy steps that led to the dark main door of the castle.

CHAPTER THIRTEEN

Miss Eells and Emerson were sitting very still on a sofa in a room with a high vaulted ceiling. Against the far wall stood a marble altar with a hideous life-sized statue of a woman. She was sitting cross-legged, and she wore a golden robe. Her skin was bright red and her bulging eyes were lifelike and red-veined. In her coiled yellow hair she wore a crescent moon. One hand held a sceptre, while the other was pointing at golden letters that said

MOYPIOI

on her forehead. High up on the wall that rose behind the statue were two niches, which held two ugly statues of giants wielding clubs. On the left was a wall that was blank except for a small oval window. In the center of the room a white china oil lamp with Dutch scenes painted on it in blue stood on a low round pedestal. The lamp was lit, and its light—though faint—seemed to reach every corner of the room. Near the lamp stood a middle-aged woman with a homely, wrinkly face and icy pale blue eyes. She was wearing a brown tweed tailored suit, and her arms were folded. A faintly amused smile curled her lips. It was Adele Grimshaw, the owner of the antique shop.

"Yes, it's me, folks," she said quietly, as she gazed at the two rigid figures on the sofa. "Good old dumpy, dowdy, unimaginative Adele. Otherwise known as Mrs. G. Warmish of thirty-eight Three Rod Road, Stillwater. It's a big surprise, isn't it? You thought I was dead. Well, as they say, things are not always what they seem. No sir-ree. That horror show in my office was staged for your benefit, so you'd think I was gone forever. I changed my name and moved up here, and got ready to play the greatest scene in my life. But you weren't willing to leave me alone, were you, Myra? Oh, no. You and that stupid, skinny boy had to come up here and poke around, and now see what has happened!'" She glared malevolently at Miss Eells. "I could have killed the two of you when you broke into my house, but I said, no, let's just scare them good and they'll never come back. But I was wrong, wasn't I? You came back, and now you'll just have to take the consequences. In a few minutes, the moon will shine through that little window up there, and I will perform some very ancient rituals, and then I won't be Adele Grimshaw any more. I'll be Ashtaroth the Mighty, and I will not have one shred of a human conscience left. You know the old saying, don't you?

> 'Conscience is a word that cowards use
> Devised at first to keep the strong in awe.'

"Well, that is certainly true, as far as I'm concerned. But when my human weaknesses are gone, I won't care much what happens to you. Or rather, I should say, Ashtaroth won't care. I wonder how she'll handle you? Fry your brains with a glance? Burn you to death with liquid fire? I really can't imagine, but I'm sure it will be memorable."

Silence fell, and Mrs. Grimshaw paced back and forth near the altar where the lamp burned. Her captives were paralyzed: They could see and hear, but they couldn't speak or move a muscle. Miss Eells wanted to scream angry insults at this evil woman, but the screams were trapped in her head. Mrs. Grimshaw glanced at her watch, and she frowned impatiently. "The moon has not risen high enough yet," she muttered, "so we still have time. I'll bet you have no idea how I found out about the powers of the lamp. Well, it so happens that there was a secret compartment in the base of the lamp, a cavity that no one knew about—no one, that is, but the late Mr. Nightwood. I found out about it when I was cleaning the lamp, and inside I found a little scroll of onionskin paper with writing on it. Only at first, you see, I didn't think all those dark shaded squiggles were writing at all. The writing was in Sanskrit, a very ancient language, and it looks like a lot of weird musical notes hanging off dark heavy bars. Needless to say, I didn't know what I had, but I've never thrown away anything valuable in my entire life. So I tucked the scroll into a drawer in my desk, and then I sold the lamp to you, Myra. But later I got curious and took the scroll to a language expert at Macalester College who translated it for me."

Mrs. Grimshaw heaved a sigh and smiled vaguely. "After that, of course, I had a problem: I had some information that could save me from the rotten unhappy life I've been living for years. You don't know what it's like, living alone and knowing that nobody cares for you. Now I had a chance to change all that, and there was the problem of the evil spirit that haunted the lamp and killed poor old Mr. Yurchak. If I tried to swipe the lamp back, the wretched thing would come after me, wouldn't it? So I thought for a while, and I finally decided to see what ancient writers had said about ghosts. I turned up a book called *De mortuis gerenda*, by St. Augustine. Probably you've come across it, Myra. You seem fairly well-read, in spite of being a flighty flibbertigibbet. At any rate, dear old Augustine had some ideas about how to handle evil spirits, and I took his advice, and it worked! Once I had my hands on the lamp, I read Augustine's incantations and sent the demon that had haunted Mr. Nightwood's tomb back into the outer darkness where it belongs." She laughed harshly. "Well, after that, I discovered that I could work wonders just by rubbing the lamp and saying some of the spells that were written on the little onionskin scroll. Knowledge and power flowed into me, and I found that I could create magical illusions. I could make it look as if I had turned to dust, I could make people think they were drowning in a well, I could fill this moldy old room with phantoms that looked like real partygoers who were having a high old time. Right now I have many of the powers of Ashtaroth, and I can do things that you wouldn't think were possible. Ah, but the best is yet to come! In a few minutes you folks are going to see something that hasn't happened in three thousand years. How lucky you are!"

At this point Mrs. Grimshaw stopped speaking and strode forward to the couch where Miss Eells and Emerson were sitting rigidly. She unbuttoned Emerson's jacket, reached inside, and popped open the compact box. Inside was the clay tablet, and it was glowing a bright cherry red. With a scornful smile, the woman squeezed it and it turned to dust, a red glittering powder that sifted out onto the floor. Then Mrs. Grimshaw walked back to the low altar where the lamp burned and turned once more to face her prisoners.

She coughed and ran her forefinger over her upper lip. "It'll be genuinely incredible," she went on in an awestruck tone. "I'll be like a god! And I'll be able to live forever. I'll have the power to kill people with a glance, and I'll push around the idiots who've been giving me a hard time all my life. Come to think of it, I won't kill the two of you. First, I'll turn this rabbity little know-it-all into an ant. He thinks he's so wonderful, well, let him try being wonderful while he's tiny and helpless and crawling on the floor. As for you, Myra . . . oh well, we can decide that later. No need to rush into these things. But it must be almost time for the moon to appear in the window, and when that happens, I have to begin the rituals that were written on that funny little scroll of paper. This is the last time that I'll be speaking to you as Adele Grimshaw, and I want to say that I'm sorry you folks got mixed up in this. But I'm not going to be responsible for what Ashtaroth does to you when she travels millions of light-years out of the dark void and inhabits my body. On the other hand, if bad things happen to snoopy people, then they only have themselves to blame. Well, here we go!"

At the far end of the enormous room, Anthony crouched behind a wooden screen. He had heard most of Mrs. Grimshaw's speech, and as he listened, he found that he was getting angrier and angrier. Then his anger died, and he felt helpless, alone, and frightened. What could he do to stop her? He wanted to rush in and beat her with his fists, but before he got anywhere near her, he would probably be paralyzed or dead. As Mrs. Grimshaw fussed with her magical objects and muttered prayers, Anthony's mind raced feverishly. What could he do? Mrs. Grimshaw was hovering over the oil lamp, and she seemed to be saying prayers to it. Anthony's hand tightened on the grip of the catapult, and the germ of an idea came floating into his head. Quickly he felt for the zippered pocket on the side of his jacket. Were they there? Ah, they were! Undoing the zipper, he reached in and took out two shiny steel ball bearings. He had carried them around for years, and sometimes he clicked them together in his hand as a sort of nervous habit. Carefully he inserted one of the ball bearings in the trough of the catapult, and then he pulled the lever back till the spring was cocked. The hand that held the catapult was shaking, and Anthony had to steady it by laying his other hand on top of it. Blood was roaring in his ears, and he bit his lip nervously. But as he crouched and waited, he knew that he was ready.

Meanwhile, Mrs. Grimshaw finished her preparations. She walked slowly and majestically to an antique chair that stood in a corner. A robe was draped across it, and she put it on. Suddenly the robe glowed with a million jeweled sparks—pearly gray, the shimmering blue and orange of an opal, dazzling diamond flashes.

With steady, solemn strides, Mrs. Grimshaw advanced toward the pedestal where the lamp burned. She bowed and then picked up a gilded censer that stood on the floor near the lamp. After spooning incense onto the glowing charcoal that burned inside the censer, she walked around the pedestal three times, swinging the smoking vessel by its chain and muttering strange words. After a pause, she put down the censer and bowed low, three times, to the staring red idol. Suddenly Mrs. Grimshaw spoke a harsh foreign-sounding word, and in answer, the fiery Greek letters on the idol's forehead burned more brightly, and tongues of fire appeared on all the walls of the room. They licked upward and cast wild leaping shadows across the ceiling, and an excited whispering began. The whispering swelled to a roar, and then Mrs. Grimshaw raised her arms, and the noise died. A pale light appeared in the oval window that was set high up on the east wall of the room. The moon was shining in, casting a long pale dusty beam on the quietly burning oil lamp. Mrs. Grimshaw raised her arms and cried aloud in a voice that filled the room:

"Come, Ashtaroth! Come Ishtar, Astarte, Spirit of the Moon, whose power of old shook the cities of the plain. Fill me with the life that will not—"

"You rotten old woman!" Anthony yelled, and with that, he raised the catapult, gripped it with both hands, took aim at the lamp, and fired. The ball bearing hit the low stone pedestal with a loud crack and rolled away into some dark corner of the room. Mrs. Grimshaw lowered her arms, and the tongues of fire on the walls died. The excited whispering was hushed.

"Is that you, you snot-nosed gangling lout?" Mrs. Grimshaw asked in a loud angry voice. "When your helicopter landed, I sensed that there were three of you, but I thought that by now you would have run away. I see that I was wrong. Well, you will have to suffer along with the others!"

Mrs. Grimshaw raised her left hand and began to speak in a strange foreign tongue. But Anthony had reloaded the catapult, and with a violent yell he stood up and fired. The ball bearing hit the chimney of the lamp and shattered it. An icy draft began to blow into the room through the doorway behind Anthony. It made the flame of the lamp flicker, and strange leaping shadows rushed back and forth across the floor. Suddenly the lamp went out, fell over on its side, and rolled off the pedestal and onto the floor. Mrs. Grimshaw's hand fell to her side, and the dazzling moon-jeweled robe became a cloak of shadows. A pool of moonlight still bathed the pedestal, and by this light Anthony saw a short hunched figure who was moving toward Mrs. Grimshaw. It was the figure of a short man in a tattered black overcoat. Mrs. Grimshaw screamed, and as Anthony watched in horror, her body was wrapped in swirls of bright fire. The screaming went on, then died, and clouds of acrid smoke filled the air. Emerson and Miss Eells found that they could move, and they leaped from their seats.

In the darkness the two suddenly released prisoners blundered about, while all around them a crashing noise rose to a thundering, drumming roar. *"This way!"* yelled Anthony. *"There's a door over here!"* A thin pencil-beam of light appeared—Anthony had pulled out his St. Christopher pocket Pen Lite, which he always carried with him, and Emerson and Miss Eells followed him through an archway and down a winding flight of stone stairs. Anthony never figured out how they got out of the burning, collapsing building, but they did. Before he knew it, they were pounding across the ice toward the helicopter, and behind them loud echoing booms filled the air. A chunk of stone shot through the sky like a meteorite and flashed into darkness on the other side of the lake. Finally they reached the helicopter, and then all three turned to look. The stone house lay in ruins, and within it a lurid cauldron of orange fire pulsed and glowed. A tall twisted column of black smoke rose into the night.

"I . . . have to . . . hand it . . . to you, Anthony," panted Emerson as he clutched at his side. "You really . . . settled that woman's hash. When you . . . smashed the lamp's chimney . . . you wrecked all of her spells." Emerson paused and swallowed twice. "Including," he went on, "the spell she got from St. Augustine's book, the one she used to get rid of the evil spirit. Of course, that spell was not a very strong or permanent one, be-cause—"

"Leave it to you to make stuffy comments at a time like this!" said Miss Eells as she tugged impatiently at her brother's sleeve. "Come on! Let's get this crate into the air before the fire melts the ice and we all drown! Hop to it, World War Two air ace! I'm freezing to death out here, and I'm sure . . ."

Her voice died and she glanced down at the small, charred object that Emerson carried in the crook of his arm. "Lord love a duck!" Miss Eells exclaimed. "Is that what I think it is, that thing you've got there?"

Emerson nodded and smiled placidly. "Yes, Myra. It's the lamp. You see, we've got one last thing to do before this strange, ghastly business is over with. But we can talk about that later. For now, I think you are right—we'd better make like a big bird and fly out of here. Climb in, the two of you, and we'll be off!"

CHAPTER FOURTEEN

At a little after four in the morning, Emerson's battered helicopter landed in the snowy field near the airport. Miss Eells and Anthony got out, and then she put on her skis and he strapped on the snowshoes once more. Together, they trekked across to Airport Road and slogged into town. There wasn't much chance of catching a cab at this hour of the morning, but Anthony didn't mind the long walk—he was not in a very big hurry to get home. All the way back in the copter he had been imagining what his mother and father would say to him, and now, as he drew nearer and nearer to home, his stomach tightened with fear. What could he say to excuse himself? As this was running through his mind,

Anthony suddenly thought that he heard the sound of a car motor. As he and Miss Eells turned and looked, a police car came rolling up. The chains on the car's tires chinked, and the red light on top flashed. The car stopped next to the two hikers, and a window rolled down. A burly red-faced policeman stuck his head out, and he eyed the two of them curiously.

"You wouldn't be Anthony Monday, by any chance, would you?" the cop asked in a gravelly voice.

"Yes . . . I . . . I am, sir," said Anthony falteringly.

"Your folks are worried sick about you," roared the cop, "an' the whole darned police force is out combin' the woods! We been up all night with dogs and search-lights and God knows what all! *Where the heck were you, anyway?*"

"I . . . I went on a helicopter ride," said Anthony. Then, quickly, he launched into the story that he and Emerson had cooked up on the ride back. It seemed that Miss Eells's brother Harlow had a farm in northern Wisconsin, and he had gotten trapped up there by the snowstorm. So Emerson had decided to fly a rescue mission up to Harlow's place, and on the way he had stopped in Hoosac to get his sister, Miss Eells. Anthony had helped them load some things on the copter, but he had fallen asleep in the back, and they had flown away, thinking Anthony was back on the ground, making his way home. By the time Anthony was discovered, they were way up north and just couldn't turn back.

". . . and that's the truth, officer, " said Anthony as he finished his tale. He swallowed hard and stared fixedly at the badge on the policeman's hat. Anthony's mother had told him many times that he got slightly cross-eyed when he lied, and he had always wondered if this was really true. Tensely, he waited for the cop to answer.

Suddenly the cop laughed and shook his head. "That has to be one of the dumbest stories I've ever heard," he growled. "I dunno if yer folks'll buy it, but that's not my problem—I'm just gonna take ya on home. And how 'bout you, Myra? Can I give you a lift?"

All through Anthony's little speech, Miss Eells had stood there with her arms folded, wondering if Officer Earl Swett would recognize her. She had known immediately who he was, of course. Officer Swett had helped Miss Eells many times in the past.

"So you've finally decided to say hello to me!" she said, cocking her head to one side and grinning wryly. "I was going to pass myself off as Ermintrude van Loon, the famous Olympic cross-country skier, but I see I've lost my chance."

"That you have, Myra," said Officer Swett, chuckling. "Now get those barrel staves off of your feet and climb in. I'd like to get to bed by dawn, if I can possibly manage it."

Miss Eells and Anthony climbed into the patrol car and rode into town. Officer Swett stopped first at the Monday house to let Anthony off, and with his snowshoes under his arm, he raced up the snowy walk. When he opened the front door he was careful not to make a lot of noise, but in the end it was no use. He had only made it halfway down the front hall when his parents appeared at the top of the stairs in their bathrobes and pajamas. At first, his mother just yelled at him. Then she burst into tears and rushed down to hug him tightly and smother his cheeks with big wet kisses. Later, when everyone had calmed down a little, Anthony told his carefully made-up story about the rescue mission to Harlow Eells's farm. The Mondays had never heard of Harlow Eells—in fact, there was no such person—but they swallowed the tale and seemed to be vaguely impressed by the fact that Anthony had gone on an errand of mercy. So peace was restored in the Monday family, but as he went to bed by the dawn's early light, Anthony wondered what Emerson was going to do about the haunted lamp.

A month passed. During that time, Miss Eells had a lot of long-distance phone conversations with her brother, and she passed on to Anthony tantalizing tidbits of information. She told him that the Swiggerts had come back to the farm where they had lived. Apparently, Mrs. Grimshaw had frightened them away so she could use the place for her own evil purposes. Also, Emerson had located the secret compartment in the lamp. A felt-covered cardboard disk was glued to the base of the lamp, and under this was a recessed space, like the hollow false bottom of a champagne bottle. And inside this space was a china disk about the size of a quarter that you could unscrew by gripping it with your fingernails. It was there that the mysterious scroll had been hidden. All this news was very interesting to Anthony, and it just made him more curious. *What* were they going to do with the lamp? Miss Eells explained that Emerson wanted to put the lamp back into the tomb where it had been, but she added that he would have to wait until the ground in Stillwater had thawed out. Workers could hack their way into the tomb with digging machines, but Emerson was afraid that the vibrations would cause the vault of the tomb chamber to collapse. So, they would just have to wait.

Early in April, Miss Eells and Anthony took a trip to Stillwater in Emerson's 1938 La Salle. They had a brief talk with the Swiggerts at their farmhouse, and then everybody went out to the grassy tomb mound that lay in a field behind the house. When he got close to the mound, Anthony saw heaps of raw yellow earth piled on one side of a long low tunnel. It was the tunnel that the robber had used. Emerson had paid some workmen to open it up again, so that he could put the lamp back where it belonged.

"Well, here we are!" said Emerson, smiling blandly and turning to his sister. He was dressed in blue jeans and a plaid cotton shirt, which made him look like a rather fussy and unlikely gentleman farmer. He wore heavy work boots and carried a bundle swathed in a piece of an old cotton blanket. "Well, how about it, Myra?" he asked teasingly. "Would you like to come in and see the demon's lair?"

Miss Eells flinched. "I'd rather be pitched headlong down a flight of stairs!" she said curtly. "If Anthony wants to be morbid and nosy, I have no objection. But I think that seeing the inside of that place would give me nightmares for a year."

"I'd like to go in with you, Mr. Eells!" said Anthony eagerly. He was dying to see what the ghastly old place looked like.

Emerson glanced quickly at the Swiggerts. They were two stout, frowny, middle-aged people, and from the looks on their faces he quickly guessed that *they* didn't want to go in. "Very well!" snapped Emerson briskly, as he turned to Anthony. "You're a good fellow, and a bulwark against the forces of darkness! Now get down on your hands and knees and follow me."

With his heart hammering, Anthony scuttled along behind Emerson. The strong smell of earth filled his nostrils, and hanging roots brushed his head. But he struggled on, and at last he reached the weird underground room. When Emerson snapped his flashlight on, Anthony took in the scene: stone walls starred with lichen and streaked with yellow niter; a warped bookcase full of moldy books; a wooden table with a magic pentacle cut into its varnished surface; a brass hand bell lying in a corner; a Bible with limp leather covers; and up against one wall, lying spread-armed, a grotesque scarecrow with buttons for eyes and a smiling mouth of red yarn.

Emerson pulled himself to his feet and played the flashlight's beam around. "Lovely place, eh?" he muttered. "By the way, our scarecrow friend here had a secret sewn into his belly—it's a can containing Mr. Nightwood's ashes. I had to do a little research to find that out, but apparently it's the truth. We have to tidy things up a bit and leave this place the way it was when the chamber was originally sealed years ago. If you help me it shouldn't take long."

For a while Emerson and Anthony scurried about the grim stone chamber, picking up things and arranging them the way they had been before the robber came. The grimy cobwebbed chair was pulled up to the table, and the Bible and bell were set in the places marked out for them in yellow chalk. Finally they dragged the rustling, limp scarecrow across the room and propped it up in the chair. As they set it in place, Anthony noticed that the scarecrow's belly had been ripped open. Probably this had been done by the robber, who was looking for treasure. Anthony shuddered. For some reason, this straw dummy seemed almost like a real corpse to him. The button eyes stared blindly, but as the flashlight's beam fell across them they almost seemed to wink.

"And now, you ask, what happens?" said Emerson

loudly as he picked the swathed bundle up off the floor. "We complete the charmed circle and make our exit."

With a flourish, Emerson whipped away the blanket. There was the lamp that had given them all so much trouble. Its base was chipped, there were scorch marks on the sides, and the chimney was gone. But it was still a lamp, and could have been filled with kerosene and lit. Carefully, Emerson set the lamp in the middle of the table . . . and then something unexpected happened. In a split second the room went black, and then a greenish halo of light grew out of nowhere and hung over the table. Instead of a scarecrow, Anthony saw the seated figure of Willis Nightwood. He sat with his flabby hands clasped before him on the table, and his beady eyes stared with demonic intensity at the lamp. A blue lightning flash seared the air, and the room went dark again. When Emerson's flashlight came on, it showed only a scarecrow seated at a table that held an oil lamp, a Bible, and a bell.

Anthony was terrified. He opened and closed his mouth, but no sound came out. When he turned and looked at Emerson, he saw to his utter amazement that the little man was totally unconcerned. He hummed quietly as he waved his flashlight beam around.

"I expected that something unusual might happen when we put the lamp back," said Emerson calmly. "Such reactions are predicted in this book I read called *On the*

Restoration of Charmed Circles. It's fascinating reading, and I recommend it to you. Now I think we had better get out of here so that Mr. Swiggert's hired man can start filling in the tunnel. After you, my dear Alphonse!"

When Anthony crawled out into the daylight again, he saw a tall gangly man standing nearby with a shovel in his hand. Miss Eells and the Swiggerts were there, too, looking anxious, but they cheered up as soon as they saw that Emerson and Anthony were all right. Emerson bounced to his feet and brushed dirt off his jeans.

"So that is that!" he said with a confident smile. "Keep this place safe from trespassers and human moles, Mr. Swiggert, and I'm sure you will not be troubled by any, er, manifestations. Shall we all go have something to eat?"

With the sound of shoveling going on in the background, the little procession wound its way back to the farmhouse. It was nearly noon, and Mrs. Swiggert had fixed a huge lunch for her guests: roast beef sandwiches with homemade bread, olives, celery, pickles, and apple pie with ice cream. Emerson had brought along several bottles of expensive champagne to drink with the meal, and he made a big deal out of popping the corks and swirling the bottles around in the elaborately decorated silver ice buckets that were stamped with his own personal monogram. Everyone sat down to eat in the sunny dining room of the old house, and for a long time the only sounds were munching and the clinking of silverware and glasses. But after a while Emerson began to notice that Miss Eells was looking rather glum. She toyed with her sandwich, and had taken only one or two sips from her wineglass.

"So what's with *you*, Myra?" said Emerson suddenly, as he set down his glass and gave his sister a beetle-browed glare. "We've survived, and we have defeated a terrible enemy who could have given the world a great deal of trouble. Isn't that enough for you?"

Miss Eells sighed. "I suppose it ought to be," she said as she tore a small piece of bread off a sandwich and popped it into her mouth. "But I can't help feeling sorry for Adele. She really had been living a crummy life, and all she wanted was a chance to be a happier person. I wonder if she really understood the chances she was taking, and the powers she was calling up out of the abyss."

Emerson sniffed disdainfully. "I wouldn't waste any sympathy on *her*!" he snapped. "She knew darned well what she was doing, and if she had been given a chance, she would have made our lives absolute hell. Believe me, I know what I'm talking about!" He took a big swig of champagne and grabbed a handful of stuffed olives from the dish in the middle of the table.

"But Mr. Eells," Anthony said, "she could've killed us when we came to this house to snoop around. I think she must've let us go because she was friends with Miss Eells."

Emerson smiled maliciously. "Friends indeed!" he said with a sarcastic toss of his head. "By the way, Myra, what was it that she called you when we were sitting paralyzed on that couch? A flighty flibbertigibbet, wasn't it?"

Miss Eells made a squinchy face. "Ye-es," she said slowly. "I do believe that is what it was." She picked up her sandwich, took a large bite, and chewed it. For some reason, it was beginning to taste better. "And furthermore, Em," she added, giving her brother a shrewd sidelong glance, "she called you something too. Do you remember what it was?"

Emerson's face got red. He picked a fork up off the table and examined it carefully. "No, Myra," he muttered. "I don't think I recall—"

"I remember!" put in Anthony suddenly. "She said you were a rabbity little know-it-all. That was it, wasn't—"

Anthony stopped talking when he saw that Emerson was glaring at him. There was a long and awkward silence, which was finally broken by Miss Eells.

"Mrs. Swiggert," she said loudly and clearly, "I'll have a large piece of pie for dessert, and two scoops of ice cream." She paused and quickly drained her wineglass. "And I think I'll have some more champagne too. I had a mild fit of indigestion, but it's passed, and now I feel like celebrating!"

JOHN BELLAIRS

is the critically acclaimed, best-selling author of many Gothic novels, including *The House with a Clock in Its Walls* trilogy, *The Curse of the Blue Figurine*; *The Mummy, the Will, and the Crypt*; *The Spell of the Sorcerer's Skull*; *The Revenge of the Wizard's Ghost*; and *The Eyes of the Killer Robot*; as well as a previous novel about Anthony Monday and Miss Eells, *The Dark Secret of Weatherend*.

A resident of Haverhill, Massachusetts, Mr. Bellairs is currently at work on another chilling tale.

FROM THE SPOOKY, EERIE PEN OF JOHN BELLAIRS . . .

☐ **THE CURSE OF THE BLUE FIGURINE**   15540/$2.95

Johnny Dixon knows a lot about ancient Egypt and curses and evil spirits—but when he finds the blue figurine, he actually "sees" a frightening, super-natural world. Even his friend Professor Childermass can't help him!

☐ **THE MUMMY, THE WILL AND THE CRYPT**   15701/$2.95

For months Johnny has been working on a riddle that would lead to a $10,000 reward. Feeling certain that the money is hidden somewhere in the house of a dead man, Johnny goes into his house where a bolt of lightning reveals to him that the house is not quite deserted . . .

☐ **THE SPELL OF THE SORCERER'S SKULL**   15726/$2.95

Johnny Dixon is back, but this time he's not teamed up with Dr. Childermass. That's because his friend, the Professor, has disappeared!

Buy them at your local bookstore or use this page to order.

BANTAM SKYLARK BOOKS

FUN AND ADVENTURE BEYOND YOUR WILDEST IMAGINATION!

☐ **JACOB TWO-TWO MEETS THE HOODED FANG**
by Mordecai Richler   **42109-1 $2.50**

Jacob is $2+2+2$ years old! But he's brave enough to rescue all the children from the clutches of the dreaded "Hooded Fang" and return from the dungeon "from which no brat returns!"

☐ **JACOB TWO-TWO AND THE DINOSAUR**
by Mordecai Richler   **15589-X $2.75**

Jacob's parents have come back from safari with a little lizard he names Dippy. Very soon, however, Dippy grows and grows into a dinosaur with a 10-ton appetite! Jacob must save him from a terrible fate in the hands of greedy grownups!

☐ **LIZARD MUSIC**
by D. Manus Pinkwater   **15605-5 $2.95**

When his parents go away for two weeks, Victor takes a vacation right at home—staying up late, watching TV, eating pizza with anchovies. In the midst of all this fun . . . he discovers a secret community of super-intelligent lizards. What follows for Victor is the adventure of a lifetime!

Buy them at your local bookstore or use this page to order:

Bantam Books, Dept. SK24, 414 East Golf Road, Des Plaines, IL 60016

Please send me the books I have checked above. I am enclosing $_____
(please add $2.00 to cover postage and handling). Send check or money order—no cash or C.O.D.s please.

Mr/Ms _____

Address _____

City/State _____ Zip _____

SK24—4/89

Please allow four to six weeks for delivery. This offer expires 10/89.
Prices and availability subject to change without notice.

Bant SK24—4/89